"But, you see, no one has ever kissed me."

Dominique didn't know what had made her say such a thing—to Presidio Romanos of all people!

Suddenly he pulled her forcibly against him. "That can soon be remedied," he announced. He bent her over his arm and she felt the sudden heat of his mouth on hers. When she tried to struggle, her feet came off the ground and she was entirely in his arms. It seemed as if he would kiss the breath right out of her body. Finally he set her down and she stood swaying, incapable of speech.

"When a girl tells a man she's never been kissed, she's asking for the obvious," he remarked.

"You know I wasn't inviting you—it just slipped out!" Dominique retorted hotly.

"Most Freudian remarks do...."

VIOLET WINSPEAR
is also the author of these

Harlequin Presents

and these

Harlequin Romances

VIOLET WINSPEAR

no man of her own

Harlequin Books

TORONTO • LONDON • LOS ANGELES • AMSTERDAM
SYDNEY • HAMBURG • PARIS • STOCKHOLM • ATHENS • TOKYO

Harlequin Presents edition published March 1982
ISBN 0-373-10492-8

Original hardcover edition published in 1981
by Mills & Boon Limited

Printed in U.S.A.

CHAPTER ONE

DOMINIQUE DAVIS stood quietly at the rail of the steamer, which was heading through waters of a shining blue.

Her abstracted gaze was framed by spectacles and her flaxen hair was drawn to the nape of her neck in a plain knot. Slowly her hands clenched the warm hardness of the railing, pressing upon it to the edge of pain. If only she were sailing to San Sabina as a holiday-maker, bent on pleasure and relaxation in the southern sun!

She sighed and envied the buoyant chatter of her fellow passengers, their eager expectations centred upon the continuing wonder of the weather and the charm of the coastline which stretched ahead of the steamer, a rambling serpentine of pale sands and dark rocks and beyond them the diverse attractions of the Italian resort.

Candice, her sister, had gone to San Sabina two years ago to become the bride of Antonio Romanos, the good-looking dancing champion whom Candy had met and attracted at a Claridge's supper dance. She had always been crazy about dancing ... now Dominique had received word that Candice lay paralysed at the house where she and Tony lived as part of the Romanos ménage. The head of the household, Don Presidio, had sent the news that Dominique's sister was afflicted and in need of her.

Yet again Dominique told herself that it couldn't be true. Candice had always been so full of life and so eager to explore all its excitements. Tony had matched her for looks and vitality and they had danced as a team until he finally persuaded his brother to agree to their marriage.

The stipulation had been that the couple return to San Sabina to be married. Dominique had been occupied at the time with her final nursing exams and it had not been possible for her to attend the wedding. But she had met Tony and had somehow felt confident that her sister would be happy with him. She had sent loving good wishes and concentrated on passing her exams, which she had done to her quiet jubilation. It had seemed at the time that both she and Candy had achieved their goal in life.

Now, two years later, came this summons and the astounding, dreadful news that Candice had lost the use of her legs . . . those long, graceful, dancing legs.

As fervently as Dominique wished to believe that nothing quite so awful could have happened to her sister, common sense told her that Don Presidio wouldn't have sent for her in such an imperative manner if the situation wasn't serious.

The words were as if stamped in the sky. *Come instantly. Your sister has a paralysis of the legs and needs you. I shall explain further upon your arrival at San Sabina.*

A feeling of apprehension wended its way through the almost too slender figure of Dominique. She had never met Tony's older brother, but in one of her letters Candice had said of him that he was an aloof man of business who, since the untimely death of the girl he had intended for his wife, had withdrawn from the society of women and gave much of his attention to the fields and vineyards which he managed for a large farming corporation.

There had been something in the tone of Candy's letters which made Dominique feel wary of her forthcoming meeting with Don Presidio. At the time of Tony's marriage to her sister there had been more than a hint of reluctance on the part of the Don. There was every possibility that he had wished his brother to bring an Italian bride into the family and Tony's choice of an English girl had met with his disapproval.

The sun struck warm across Dominique's strained features, but she didn't feel it, blinking slightly as the brightness sheened the surface of her spectacles. Tony was wonderfully charming and she could understand why her sister had fallen in love with him, but that brother of his sounded as if he might be a bit of a tyrant. Dominique didn't like to be uncharitable, so she told herself that perhaps he had buried his heart with his fiancée and took a sour view of love when he saw it in others.

As Dominique disembarked with the other passengers her heart felt weighted by anxiety and the need to get to her sister's side. The radiant atmosphere of San Sabina was lost upon her. She failed to notice the speckless sky and the scent of citrus in the yards of the white-walled houses rambling up the hillsides. She went through the formalities of landing on Italian soil in an automatic way, unaware that as a woman alone she was being quizzed with some curiosity.

'The *signorina* visits San Sabina for the first time?'

Dominique came out of her reverie and found one of the Italian officers looking at her in a speculative kind of way; it flitted across her mind that had Candice been standing here with the sunlight in her hair there would have been admiration in the man's eyes.

'Yes, this is my first visit.' She replied to him in quite good Italian, for it was one of the languages she

had chosen to study when her sister married Tony
Romanos. 'I believe I'm being met by a servant from
the house of Don Presidio Romanos.'

'Ah, the *signorina* is a guest of the Don?' The offi-
cer's eyes ran over the simple lines of her dove-grey
suit, her silver initial affixed to the lapel.

'Does he live far from here?' she asked.

'Some miles inland.' His manner had undergone a
subtle change, as if mention of the Romanos family
placed her in the category of people to be treated with
a restrained respect.

'Do you know the Romanos family?' she asked
curiously.

'Everyone here in San Sabina knows of them.' Her
passport was returned with a cool politeness. 'I hope
your stay will be an enjoyable one, *signorina*.'

'*Grazie*.' Enjoyment was not what she was expecting
to find here, and as Dominique walked away from the
desk her heart felt heavier than the suitcase which she
carried out into the hot sunlight, there to stand and
look about for a man in a chauffeur's uniform. Again it
stole through her mind that someone would have leapt
to carry her suitcase had she been Candice, and several
young men would have been clamouring to give her a
lift. Dominique's smile was faintly quizzical. It had
always been that way for Candice, she had never lacked
male attention, whereas Dominique had always gone
without it.

Except upon this occasion, for as other people from
off the steamer were wafted away in cabs and buses,
Dominique found herself being stared at from several
yards across the pavement by a tall, intensely dark-
haired man whose eyes sent a most curious sensation
all the way down her spine . . . eyes that were startling
in that dark face, for they were like icy silver as they

caught and held her gaze.

Dominique fought to evade his scrutiny; he wasn't in a driver's uniform, so he wasn't from the Romanos house. Firmly she turned her back on him, but she knew from the reaction of her skin when he came and stood directly behind her, though he had made no sound as he crossed the pavement. Dominique wasn't usually a nervous person, but right now she found herself tensed in every atom of her body. It was a feeling she didn't like and she spun to face the man in case he dared to lay his hands upon her.

'What do you want?' In her nervousness she spoke in English.

'You—I imagine.'

'How dare—you'd better leave me alone!' He seemed even darker and taller close to her and she backed several paces away from him. 'I—I'm related to the Romanos family and the Don doesn't take kindly to—to your type of person!' she blurted.

'And what, pray, is my type of person?' His eyes scanned her every feature, lingering on the owlish frames of her glasses.

'A wolf,' his look had brought the colour into her cheeks, 'who preys upon women on their own. If you're after my purse, then you won't get much! Go on, leave me alone before the chauffeur from the Romanos house arrives—there might be trouble.'

'Do I look as if a chauffeur might make me tremble in my shoes?' A smile flickered around his lips. 'I don't take orders from a woman, least of all your sort.'

'My—sort?' Her flush deepened and seemed to burn her skin; she knew what he meant, she was plain and unglamorous, and whatever his motive in approaching her, it wasn't in order to make a pass at her.

'You don't know the first thing about men—about

life, come to that.'

'Th-thank you for the character reading!'

'You are welcome, *signorina*.' One of his black brows had a sardonic angle to it. 'How quaint are some of you English women. You are either stretched out on our beaches in just a coat of sun oil, or you are acting as if Queen Victoria still rules your every thought and action.'

'Well—really!' Dominique had very little experience in dealing with men, and this one really confounded her. 'Who do you think you are?'

'Didn't you say I was a wolf who preys upon lonely women?'

'Yes.' She said it defiantly and yet felt disconcerted by the way he looked, as if wryly amused by everything about her.

'Women will sometimes go to extremes, is that not so?'

'I—I suppose they do.' Gripping the handle of her suitcase, Dominique started to move away from him, wishing the Romanos driver would appear and whisk her swiftly away from this Italian whose looks and remarks were so annoying.

'Miss Davis, I agree that the joke has gone far enough.'

She almost stumbled, then taking a deep breath she slowly turned to study him more closely . . . the boldly shaped nose and mouth, and strong clefted chin. The well cut grey suit and wine-coloured shirt, a pearl grey tie exactly knotted under the tailored collar of the shirt. Added to which, she realised, was the fact that he had been speaking to her in perfect English, his accent providing just a touch of the exotic.

'Who are you?' she exclaimed, even though a suspicion had already struck a nerve.

'I am Don Presidio Romanos.' He announced it with a touch of arrogance. 'And you are the sister of Candice—I see no vagrant likeness, even your eyes are a different colour.'

'We never were alike, but I assure you, *signore*, we are sisters.' It had been said before and it always meant the same, why was Candy so pretty and why was Dominique so plain?

'My sister, *signore*—please tell me how she is!'

'You are naturally perturbed about her.'

'I'm extremely troubled—I want to know exactly what has happened.'

'We will proceed to the car and I will tell you what has occurred as we drive to the Villa Dolorita.'

'Why is Candice at your house instead of a hospital——?'

'Come,' he took her suitcase with one hand and clasped her elbow with the other, 'my car is parked just around the corner.'

Dominique had no choice but to let him propel her in the direction of an armour-toned car built for speed. The seats were low and comfortable and there was a tang of cigar smoke, a rich blend that went with the Don's fine suiting; the assured style of the man.

She was aware that some people carried within them the essence of their breeding, and she winced at the way she had accused him of being a wolf who preyed upon lonesome women.

Quite soon they had left the town behind them and were driving along a narrow road, winding in a ribbon around a crag of land that seemed to have its summit in the cerulean blue sky.

Candice had never described San Sabina except to say that it was picturesque. It also seemed to Dominique to be rather wild, especially this region

which they had entered, one side of the road a sheer
drop to where the ocean spilled back and forth, licking
greedily at the immense rocks that jutted out of the
silvery sand. It was wildly dramatic scenery and at any
other time Dominique would have been enthralled by
it, but her thoughts and her concern were taken up by
her sister and with anxious impatience she waited for
Don Presidio to explain matters.

'I expect it came as a shock to you, Miss Davis, to
be informed so bluntly about your sister's condition?'
He spoke in a reserved tone of voice, in which she
detected a certain lack of feeling.

'I was considerably shocked,' she agreed.

'After consideration it seemed the best way to inform
you—the quick dose of bitter medicine rather than the
sweet pill.'

'Very hard to swallow, *signore*, especially as I
assumed that all was well with Candice.'

'She had not written to you at any time to let you
know of her mishap?'

'Mishap?' Dominique caught her breath. 'Surely
more than that if, as you say, she has lost the use of
her legs!'

'You had no idea anything was wrong until you
received word from me, *signorina*?'

'None! The last time I saw Candy she was in excellent health. She's all the family I have and I care very
much about her, even though she lives here in Italy
and we see each other infrequently.'

'As a Latin I have the understanding of the bonds
that bind brothers together and link sisters to each
other. May I remark that you and your sister appear to
be different types?'

'We are,' Dominique agreed. 'But we care about
each other—I care!'

'I am gratified that you came to San Sabina without delay. So far your sister has worn out the patience of five nurses, so I'm hoping that you will have better luck with her.'

'You want me to stay and nurse her?'

'If that is possible?'

'I was due to go on a case, but I cancelled it in order to come here to Candice—there have been five nurses already?'

'Five,' he said succinctly.

'I don't understand—my sister was never a disagreeable person.'

'She has now become most difficult.' He took a curve of the road at confident speed. 'She screams abuse at her husband and blames him for the way she is.'

'How on earth did it happen?' Dominique's gaze was fixed upon the defined Latin profile and she told herself again that he was a hard man.

'It happened, *signorina*, because Candice chose to believe that my brother had betrayed her. They had a flaming argument out on the *terrazza* at the rear of the villa—he had given her a string of pearls and she accused him of buying them in order to salve his conscience. Candice struck him across the face with the pearls and the clasp cut his lip. In the heat of temper Tony struck back at her and in backing away from him your sister lost her footing and fell down a flight of stone steps. She was knocked unconscious and rushed by ambulance to hospital——'

'Why wasn't I informed of all this?' Dominique felt a sharp quiver of anger go through her. 'I had the right to be told——'

'Her injuries, Miss Davis, weren't considered serious. She had a lot of bruising and a slight concussion from where she struck her head on the flagstones, but within twenty-four hours she was out of hospital and I decided——'

'*You* decided? Surely it was up to Tony——?'

'My brother was greatly upset by the occurrence. I discussed with him the matter of informing you, but Candice improved so rapidly that it seemed un-neccessary to drag you away from your work. I do assure you, *signorina*, there was every sign that your sister was making a good recovery from her mishap ... until she stepped from her bed one morning and collapsed. One of the best doctors was called in on her case and he took considerable pains to get to the cause of the trouble, and his decision was that the root of it lay in her mind, not her body.'

Dominique looked at him with disbelief. 'Are you implying that Candice is suffering from hysterical paralysis?'

'I'm not implying it, *signorina*, I am stating it as a fact.' He seemed to bite the words with his hard white teeth. 'Her legs are useless because she wishes to play the martyr.'

'Oh, it isn't fair to say such a thing!' Dominique couldn't associate the person Don Presidio spoke about with the sister she had always known, lovely and loving, with a kind of glamour about her. 'You're saying that her motive is to make Tony feel responsible and guilty!'

'Yes.' He didn't hesitate to admit it. 'She wants to punish him—she wants it so much that she has allowed her hysteria to find the means. Her ability to dance brought them together, did it not? Their mutual admir-ation for each other was centred in that, so she strikes back at him by losing the ability to dance. Whenever they are together she can accuse him of being the cause of her invalidism, and naturally he believes it.'

'These implications about him—that he had betrayed Candice. Have they any foundation, *signore*?'

'I don't believe so.'

'Can you be certain?'

'Before his marriage my brother had wild oats to sow, but I'm confident that he has been faithful to your sister.'

'Candice couldn't have felt your confidence in him, *signore*, not if they had a fight which led to her falling down a flight of stone steps. Poor Candy!'

'Your concern does you credit, Miss Davis, but what of my poor brother? Tony is at his wits' end to know how to deal with her and the situation in which he finds himself.'

'He could be as guilty as sin.' Dominique just had to say it. 'He's your brother, so naturally you defend him, but you never fully approved of their marriage, did you? Perhaps you hoped to choose Tony's wife—the arranged marriage is still a tradition in Italy, isn't it?'

'*Si*, but if I had reservations about Tony's marriage it was simply that I felt he was still rather young emotionally.'

'I can't say he struck me that way,' Dominique argued.

'What would a girl like you know about it?'

She flushed. 'I thought he had charm and good manners, but I—I can't say the same about you!'

'I am mortified.'

'You're arrogant——' Dominique bit her lip, for it went against her principles to make hasty judgments about people, but this man did have an abrasive effect on her. Here she was, on the verge of quarrelling with him even as poor Candice lay in his house with something seriously amiss with her. It might even be true that she had retreated into some kind of shell in which to play the invalid was her way of punishing Tony for a real or fictional sin.

'The doctor's quite certain that Candy's condition isn't due to some injury to the spine connected with her fall?' Dominique's voice shook with anxiety.

'His examinations were thorough. X-rays of your sister's body revealed no fractures or distortions to account for her inability to walk. She has certainly lost the use of her legs, but the conclusion has to be that the condition is self-induced. Distressing for her, and equally distressing for you to hear, *signorina*, but there is no way to cushion the feelings when it comes to disagreeable news.'

'Because I'm a spinster it doesn't mean that I need to be cushioned against the facts of life, *signore*. My work as a nurse confronts me with all sorts of people and their problems.'

'Nonetheless to hear this about your sister has been a blow, eh?'

'Yes,' she sighed. 'I've never associated hysteria with Candice. She's always been so outgoing and carefree. She has often chided me for my seriousness.'

'*Si*, to be a spinster wouldn't suit Candice.' He spoke in the droll tones of a man to whom women—most women—were an open book.

Dominique sat there silently and felt tiny curlings of fear inside her. She remembered the almost feverish glow about Candice when she had first met Tony Romanos. She had talked of nothing else but the way he affected her, like too much wine, intoxicating her.

'It's true that Candice adores your brother,' she murmured, and her grey eyes were very reflective. 'I believe she loved him from the first moment they danced together.'

'You sound as if you can't quite believe that such a thing could happen.'

Dominique felt the glance that raked her profile. 'Need I say, *signore*, that I have other things to think about.'

'Things of more importance, eh? In your estimation.'

'Important to me.'

'So you might think. Your sister felt these emotions and you are of the same flesh and bone.'

'Candice never had the urge to have a career, *signore*. I did.'

'Do you consider that having a career safeguards a woman from making a man the centre of her existence?'

'It wasn't for that reason——'

'I daresay others have asked, but what exactly was your reason?'

'I felt I had to find a purpose in life.' Dominique was aware that she spoke with a touch of primness, but she took pride in that purpose. 'My sister was always so attractive and she revelled in having a good time. I never condemned her for that, it was just that we held different views on life.'

'She considered love the purpose of life, eh?'

'It would seem so.'

'But for you it's serving the sick?'

'My work means everything to me.'

'Admirable,' he murmured. 'So you have forsworn life's pleasures?'

'I have sworn to serve whoever has need of my skill as a nurse.'

'Setting aside the romantic dreams most women have?'

'I—I was never a dreamer, *signore*.'

'No? Yet you have the dreamer's eyes, *signorina*.'

'W-what do you mean?' Her hands folded tightly together as she spoke.

'They are grey like the wings of a pigeon and they take flight from the gaze of a man—are you afraid that your soul might be looked into?'

'Through horn-rimmed spectacles?' She spoke drily but found his remarks very disconcerting. 'You seriously wish me to nurse Candice?'

'You are a trained nurse,' he replied, 'and while this condition of hers persists she must have someone to take care of her. She isn't proving a pliable patient, and as I told you, five nurses have already taken exception to her behaviour and taken themselves off to calmer sickrooms. However, she may permit you to take care of her. I hope so!'

'You sound as if you threaten her, *signore*.' Dominique glanced at his profile and it looked very Roman and defined, perhaps to be admired upon a bronze coin but an indication that he wasn't a man to be trifled with on any issue.

'If your sister continues to behave as if she's deranged, then I shall have her placed where they put the deranged—you catch your breath, as if in protest, but I assure you I'm a man of my word.'

'I can see that, Don Presidio, but Candice is your brother's wife and neither he nor I would permit you to do such an outrageous thing!'

'There are limits, let me tell you, to what a man will take from a wife, and if that sister of yours continues to rant and rave at Tony each time he enters her bedroom, or to indulge in orgies of weeping, he will be grateful if I drop her into the Tiber. Do I make myself understood?'

'With extreme clarity,' Dominique assured him. 'It

doesn't seem to occur to you that Candice is a very frightened girl. If she believed she was losing Tony before her accident, what must be the state of her mind now she finds herself unable to walk? You talk about self-induced paralysis as if a good spanking would cure her. You know different from that, *signore*.'

'I daresay I do,' he admitted. 'But she can be very trying, and she doesn't help herself by getting into such states of temper which when they subside have a resemblance to manic depression.'

'Wouldn't you be in a state of despair, Don Presidio, if you believed yourself to be paralysed?'

'Your sister has been told again and again that she is not a victim of paralysis. She has been shown the X-rays and had them explained to her, but nothing seems to shake her out of her conviction. Her mind is fixed upon the idea that her fall has left her crippled.'

'Poor Candy!' Apprehension curled its cold fingers around Dominique's heart. That such a catastrophe should befall her sister, who had seemed the very last person to suffer with her nerves! Perhaps she had idealised Tony too much and expected such devotion from him that even to see him smile at another woman would seem like a betrayal.

The kind of love which held Candice in thrall was a kind of mystery to Dominique, but now she spared a moment to consider what it must be like for a woman to find herself absorbed body and soul by a man. It seemed incredible to her, like giving all the Christmas gifts to one child instead of sharing them out so each child could clutch lovingly a doll or a teddy-bear.

Good heavens, how dangerous and selfish this love that could turn a vibrant and energetic girl into a neurotic invalid! Love, Dominique told herself, was a tiger she didn't want to meet in the dark!

'I'm sorry, *signorina*, that your visit to San Sabina should be overclouded in this way.'

'I'm sorry as well, *signore*.' A bleakness stole into Dominique's eyes. 'Have we much farther to go to the villa?'

'We are almost there.'

She was glad and at the same time nervous of seeing Candice. Dominique realised how long it had been since they had actually been in each other's company. They wrote the occasional letter to each other, and there had been a flying visit from the couple last Christmas. Candice had seemed perfectly all right then, laughing and glowing in her furs, cuddling up to Tony and holding his hand as if they were still honeymooners. They had taken Dominique to Claridge's for lunch and there had seemed no cloud of any sort on their horizon.

Dear God, what had gone wrong for them? Had he strayed into the arms of another woman, and was his brother protecting the family name? Or did someone dislike Candice enough to impart a malicious lie to her?

'How did Candice come to hear these stories about Tony?' she asked.

'In the form of anonymous letters. The first one she tore up, but I saw the second one and the details it contained. Your sister wouldn't accept my assurance that the letter was no more than the outpourings of a poisonous pen.'

'Why—why wouldn't Candice be reassured?' Dominique felt an almost desperate need to know. 'There had to be a reason.'

'Quite, and it related to a scar which Tony acquired only a short while after they were married. They honeymooned in the West Indies, as you know; one evening they were invited to a party where limbo dancing was taking place. Taking into account my brother's passion for any form of dancing, you'll realise that he couldn't resist competing against one of the local champions. You are aware,' the Don paused and quirked an eyebrow as if questioning Dominique's awareness, 'that in that form of exercise a flame is applied to the limbo bar and the contestants have to snake their hips beneath the flaming bar without getting burned. *Presto*, my brother went and burned himself upon a portion of his lower body ... you comprehend?'

'It must have been painful.' A vagrant smile came and went in Dominique's grey eyes. 'Surely the scar must be visible when he wears bathing trunks?'

'Tony avoids the sea—did you not know? He nearly drowned as a child, at the time our parents were lost when the *Conte Toro* went down in the Adriatic. I was away at boarding school; Tony was a mere infant and he was taken on the cruise along with his nanny. It was she who saved his life, Malina whom you will meet at the villa. Be warned that she speaks her mind, a privilege of loyal servants in Italy.'

'And what shall I be in your household, Don Presidio?' Suddenly Dominique felt quite urgent about the matter. 'Am I to be regarded as the new nurse, or as a member of the household?'

'Which would you prefer, *signorina*?' The ironic intonation in his voice was very apparent as he asked the question. 'Don't hesitate to be frank with me.'

'I think it might be better if I'm regarded as the nurse rather than your brother's sister-in-law. In which case, *signore*, I shall not expect to take meals with the family nor to participate in social activities.'

'Very well, if that is your preference.' He didn't

argue with her and a few minutes later Dominique felt
the pull of gravity as the car mounted a gradient leading to tall iron gates set between the plant-shaded walls
of a rambling house.

'We arrive at the Villa Dolorita.' There was an
unmistakable note of pride in the Don's voice, and as
the car entered the great courtyard Dominique caught
her breath and understood why he felt as he did about
the place.

In the glow of the declining sun it seemed like a
house of gold, dominating its own hilltop, sprawled
there like a noble reminder of days gone by when the
Medici dukes had ruled in Italy and men of adventure
had gone seeking their fortunes so they could buy land
and power of their own.

The villa of the Romanos family was fabulous. It
emerged as if out of some strange dream which
Dominique had not expected ... a dream over-
shadowed by the thought of Candice confined behind
those walls of beaten gold, unable to walk ... unable
to dance in the arms of the Italian husband whom she
perhaps loved a little too much.

Dominique slid from the car a moment before Don
Presidio could extend a hand to assist her.

'How admirably independent you are, *signorina*.'
With a dark eyebrow at a sardonic angle he stood
there, the flame-tinged sunlight striking across the lean
distinction of his face.

To Dominique it was a face such as the conquering
Romans must have had, forceful and demanding, with
just a shading of melancholy around the bold mouth.

'I am, *signore*,' she replied. 'The strength to be
independent lies in my vocation.'

'Are you never lonely?' He asked the question in
almost a sombre tone of voice.

'Aren't all of us alone?'

'I suppose we are. There's something a little sad in the realisation, is there not?'

He glanced about him with those eyes, dark and yet giving the illusion of the silvery ice that locks up the lakes in wintertime. It seemed to Dominique that he was searching for something he had lost . . . his young love, perhaps?

'Come, let me escort you into the villa. Come see your sister, and try not to be too disturbed by the change in her.'

Dominique's heart sank at his words, and his look, and she adroitly avoided the touch of his hand as she fell into step at his side.

CHAPTER TWO

THE Villa Dolorita was built on three levels, remote and dominant. Its vistas had been chosen with immense care and the house had grown out of the stone and tile and labour of the land itself. Each of its parts had a naturalness that was like the branches of a noble tree, or the features of a beautiful face. It had weathered the years with grace and strength, and Dominique felt moved by the ineffable charm of the villa.

She walked with the Don up a flight of mosaic steps leading to a *terrazza* from which breathtaking views of the sea and the mountains could be enjoyed. 'There below,' he said, 'far below lies the Baia d'Argento.'

'The Bay of Silver,' she murmured, and felt almost dizzy as she gazed down upon the dazzling light on the water, lucent and dancing. 'Whoever chose this site must have been a poet or a painter!'

'He was a soldier, *signorina*.'

She glanced upwards and a smile flicked at the Don's lips. '*Si*, a soldier of fortune. All of this sprang from sword and flame, not from the pen of a poet or the brush of a painter. Are you disappointed?'

She shook her head. 'I'm unsurprised.'

'Because you think you see in me the pillager rather than the poet?'

With a will of their own her eyes looked him up and down. Her first alarmed impression of him remained, the fact that he was Tony's brother did not diminish her sense of threat. This was a man whom no woman could ever take for granted ... to take Presidio Romanos for granted would be like poking an unwary hand through the bars of a tiger's cage.

All around the *terrazza* wall were big earthenware pots in which plants trailed their leaves and flowers; mauve, pink and honey-gold bells, side by side with aromatic herbs. An arched entrance led into a big cool *salone*, and there the Don informed Dominique that he was going to hand her over to a *domestica* who would show her to her room where she could freshen up and prepare herself for her meeting with Candice.

'Very well, *signore*.' She didn't argue with him; the journey had been a lengthy one and she needed to compose herself so that when she greeted her sister she would, she hoped, be in control of her emotions. Seeing a devitalised Candice was going to be shocking.

A maid answered the summons of the bell and Dominique followed her up a wide, branching staircase of elegant proportions. The villa had looked imposing on the outside and she now discovered that it was also rather grand on the inside. Not that the interior had a look of ostentation. The furnishings, in fact, had a distinct look of age and wear, but of the caring sort, so there was a patina on the rich old woods, expert darnings in the brocade drapes, and faded but speckless roses in the carpets.

It was a house which had been lived in rather than possessed. A long line of Romanos men had carried their brides over its threshold and young feet had scuffed the carpets, women had sat and gossiped in the brocaded chairs, and men had lounged around with their cigars and discussed the problems relating to their farms and vineyards.

Here in these rooms people had whispered and shouted, had loved and hated, been born and died.

Dominique's awareness of all this was occasioned by her own lack of a family upbringing. Her mother had died when Candice was only a few weeks old, and their father, an importer of Far Eastern goods such as silk, ivory, rattan and brassware, had gone suddenly to live in Singapore and had taken his infant daughters with him. Unfortunately the climate had disagreed with Candice, and the next thing Dominique clearly remembered was that they had been placed in the care of the Sisters at the House of Saint Anselma. Kindly women but with other children on their hands so that loving affection had to be shared, as toys and books were shared, until it became their way of life, its impersonal aspects accepted.

The visits of their lean, tanned father had diminished over the years, then Sister Superior had called them to her office one day and told them that he had married a young Asian woman and had settled permanently in the East. This meant that the sisters, Dominique two years older than Candice, saw him only once more after his marriage. When they were in their teens his letters ceased to arrive and they had to accept that his life out East excluded them.

It was then that Dominique began to lean towards the idea of entering the Holy Order of Saint Anselma. Candice had no such intention and found work outside the convent when she was old enough to leave. She had tried to persuade Dominique to join her in the pursuit of enjoyment. Life was to be savoured not spent in a kind of chastity belt, the keys to fun and joy thrown away. Dominique had merely smiled and as was her habit pushed at the frames of the spectacles she had worn since a child, her eyes having been found myopic by the Sisters.

She decided to begin her training as a nurse, often joining the Sisters at Saint Anselma in order to prepare herself for the day when she decided to enter the Order as an active member, which would mean the taking of novitiate vows.

At no time did she try and impose her decision upon Candice. There was a glow and an eagerness about Candy which she sensed had to find its outlet in sensuous enjoyments rather than aesthetic ones. Dominique understood, but hoped at the same time that her sister wouldn't be reckless with her gifts of beauty and gaiety. Then she had met Tony Romanos and each time the sisters met she had been glowing with love and admiration for her Italian boy-friend. They danced as one! They enjoyed the same things! He was marvellous to be with and she'd just die if he didn't ask her to marry him!

Dominique had listened and wondered a little at these exaggerated vows of love and longing. 'No one dies from love,' she smiled. 'I'm sure you have other boy-friends who dance as well as he does.'

'There's only one Tony,' Candice had sighed. 'You

just don't understand, Nicky, you're so wrapped up in taking care of sick people—not to mention all that other piety! How can you want to look like a crow?'

'Well, let's say an owl.' Dominique's sense of humour had risen above the irreverence. 'Some Orders are already discarding the habit, and Saint Anselma's might do the same one day.'

'*Signorina!*'

Dominique gave a start and realised that the maid was waiting for her to enter one of the large bedrooms. She drew her gaze from a suit of sable armour in an angle of the corridor; it stood about the same height as Don Presidio and its closed visor was somehow typical of him. She walked into the room that was to be hers and caught her breath in amazement. In a bed that size she'd be lost! And just look at the high, carved ceiling! They made her feel rather out of place, for her room at the hostel was so functional, with a narrow bed, a table and chair and a curtained recess where she hung her clothes.

Dominique had grown used to austerity and she stood in the centre of this Italianate bedroom as if poised for flight from all that it represented, comfort and coddling and maids to run up and down stairs in order to make the Romanos family and friends as comfortable as possible.

'There's no need to unpack my suitcase.' Dominique said, for the the maid had placed it upon a stool and was trying the locks.

'I shall be pleased to do it for the *signorina*.' The woman gave her a rather startled look; it was obviously one of her duties to unpack for the Don's guests.

'It won't take me more than a few minutes, and remember I'm the new nurse here. I don't expect to be waited upon hand and foot.' She was determined to make that clear, and she also wanted to establish a certain amount of distance between herself and Don Presidio. The man had a disturbing manner and she didn't like his attitude towards Candice, whom he seemed to regard as a tiresome burden upon his brother.

'Would the *signorina* like a pot of coffee brought to her?' the maid enquired.

'*Grazie*, that would be kind of you.'

The maid smiled and left the room, closing the door quietly behind her. Despite Dominique's assertion that she was the new nurse, she realised that the Don's staff would find it difficult to dissociate her from her relationship to Candice. To them she was part of the family, and she found herself wondering if it was going to be altogether easy to balance her role of nurse and sister-in-law to the second son of the house.

When her few belongings were unpacked Dominique wandered to one of the tall windows and watched the sun setting over the ocean. She hadn't dreamed that the villa was like this, a kind of isolated sea castle far from the bustle and grime of city life. The sort of life Dominique faced most days of her life, for most of her work was carried out in the poorer parts of London, her duties being those of a visiting nurse.

As the sky filled with gold, crimson and pools of blue, she let her thoughts dwell upon Tony, who had brought Candice to live in this fabulous house a long way from the noise and excitement of dance halls. As he didn't appear to work for a living Dominique presumed that he had a private income either supplied by his more industrious brother or bequeathed to him when his parents so tragically lost their lives when the *Conte Toro* caught fire in the night, so that panic as

well as flames swept the cruise ship from stem to
stern.

Tony's life had been saved by the nanny, the woman
named Malina who still lived at the villa.

A thoughtful look stole into Dominique's eyes . . .
was it remotely possible that Malina might harbour a
grudge against Candice? Did she perhaps feel that she
had some special hold upon Tony because she had
saved him from a nightmare death when the cruiser
sank in flames, taking so many other lives with it, including those of his mother and father?

Tony had survived because of Malina's courage and
devotion; now Tony was the husband of a young and
beautiful English girl!

Dominique was so lost in her thoughts that she failed
to hear the bedroom door open and was unaware of a
presence in her room. 'Our sunsets are always spec-
tacular.' The voice came from just behind her and with
a stifled cry she spun round and found herself looking
upwards into the mercurial eyes of Don Presidio.

'I did knock a couple of times,' he said. 'Finally I
looked in upon you and found you transfixed by the
sun dying over the water. It's a view I have from my
own windows and I never fail to find myself in awe of
nature's talent as an artist. I've often wished that I
could transfer such a scene on to canvas.'

The sun had gone abruptly and dusk had entered
Dominique's room along with the Don. 'Would you
like to have been an artist?' she found herself asking
him.

'A sculptor perhaps.' His teeth glimmered in a brief
smile. 'Not in stone but in bronze, and I would have
chosen to sculpt wild life, the creatures who steal from
their dens to find food when darkness falls. What does
the night mean to you, *signorina*?'

'Dim lights, white beds and the tang of medication. A restless cough perhaps, a clock ticking away on a wall and a radiator gurgling.'

'Ah, the vigilant night of a nurse.'

'Yes, *signore*.'

'You have sat through many of them?'

'A fair number. I began my training when I was seventeen.'

'I see.' His gaze was intent. 'May I remark, *signorina*, that you don't look twenty-five.'

'Woman who wear glasses are thought to look more than their age.'

'It isn't so in your case—you have an unworldly look.'

'Perhaps being brought up in a convent had something to do with it.'

'Or perhaps you had it from the beginning—you would appear to be different in several respects from your sister.'

'Candice is the beautiful one,' Dominique pointed out.

'Do you mind very much?'

'I don't mind at all,' she said sincerely. 'We are what we are and we make the most of it.'

'A brave philosophy, Miss Davis, but most women would give a lot to be born beautiful.'

'I daresay a daisy would sooner be a rose, *signore*, but a daisy it will be until its petals wither and fall.'

'Is that your own expectations, to wither on the stem until you fall?'

'I hope to be of service until I fall.'

'You have the spirit of a salvationist, *signorina*,' he drawled.

'I hope so, *signore*. I plan something in that direction.'

'Ah, may I be curious?'

'By all means, Don Presidio.' She paused, not just to create an effect but because what she had to impart was meaningful to her. 'I hope to join the Order of Saint Anselma in due course; it was where Candice and I were reared among the Holy Sisters.'

'*Santo Dio!*' he exclaimed.

'I'm quite determined, *signore*.'

'I'm sure you are.' He gave a sardonic laugh. 'I'm sure many girls of your disposition have felt the call to holy arms.'

'And what is my disposition, may I ask?' Dominique felt angered that he should mock her; how dare this man take it upon himself to question her way of life! He was a stranger to her, a man she hadn't met until today, so how dared he take it upon himself to throw doubt upon her vocation? Towering over her in this dusk-filled room he seemed like some dark inquisitor.

'I think you have a little too much compassion in your nature,' he said deliberately.

'How can anyone be too compassionate, Don Presidio, in a world whose values are rotting away? Some of us must try——'

'You are beating your heart against a stone wall.'

'It's my heart—my choice, *signore*. You have no business to be my inquisitor—unless that is your natural disposition?'

'You think I'm curious and prying, *signorina*?'

Dominique hesitated, and then temper flared up in her and she had to speak her mind. 'You think that the privileges of wealth and position give you the right to run other people's lives. Tony opposed you by wanting my sister for his wife and because of that you are hard towards her.'

'Perhaps I am a naturally hard man.'

'We have only recently met, Don Presidio, but I have formed that opinion of you.'

He inclined himself in a faintly mocking bow. 'Do you think our opinion of each other will prevent us from being—friends?'

'I'm here in your house, *signore*, as my sister's nurse. I'd like you to take me to her.'

'Are you feeling composed?' he enquired.

'Quite, thank you.'

'I thought I might have discomposed you.'

'Not at all. Is Candice expecting me?'

'No.'

'I beg your pardon!'

'She's inclined to get worked up, so she wasn't told of your impending arrival. There was always the chance that you might have had to delay your visit, and that would have disappointed her. You see, I am not cast iron.'

It seemed to Dominique that he was cast in a very unbending mould; that anyone who set themselves against him would get badly bruised in the process.

'I still think I should have been sent for at the time Candice fell down those steps and had to go into hospital,' she said. 'It was rather high-handed of you to exclude me—oh, I don't doubt that Tony was upset and uncertain about what to do, but I have my rights, you know.'

'As I told you, there was no indication at the time of anything more than cuts and bruises and a slight concussion——'

'Any kind of concussion can be unpredictable,' Dominique broke in. 'I had every right to be with my sister, but it would seem that you make all the family decisions and you decided that I'd be more of a hindrance than a help. On what did you base that assumption, may I ask?'

'Your sister's personality.'

'What do you mean?'

'Hasn't she always been a person to swing very high, or very low?'

'And you assumed that I might be the same?'

'Perhaps so.'

'That I'd become hysterical when faced with a crisis? You seem to have a poor opinion of women, *signore*, but as you can see I don't take after my sister and I do know how to keep a cool clear head in a crisis.'

'So it would seem.'

'Your brother had met me; you could have asked Tony for his opinion—if you ever stoop to asking other people for an opinion.'

'I don't happen to consider my brother the shrewdest judge of women.'

'That is a double-edged reply, *signore*. Does it imply that you consider his judgment of Candice to be to his disadvantage? I do apologise for my sister and myself for not being Italian women. No doubt you consider that they possess all the virtues—as your girl must have done!'

The moment Dominique spoke those words she regretted them. They were not only insolent, they were thoughtless and cruel. He had lost his fiancée a number of years ago, but he had never replaced her, an indication that he found his girl Amatrice hard to forget. Dominique was usually so careful of the feelings of others and she felt a tide of shame sweep over her.

'Forgive me——' she began.

'Forget it.' He swung on his heel. 'Your sister will now be awake in readiness for her tea. One afternoon, you know, she hurled the teapot clear through the window—fortunately it was open.'

'I can't imagine Candice behaving so—irrationally.'
He was striding hard along the corridor and
Dominique almost had to run to keep up with him.

'You seem convinced that your sister is the victim of
my tyranny.' The look he shot at her when he came to
a halt in front of one of the doors was icy cold. 'Perhaps
you are letting your imagination run away with you.'

Like other nurses Dominique had sometimes been
flayed by the sarcastic tones of a superior, but she had
never felt so put in her place as she felt right now. And
it was deserved, she had to admit. Like a child being
rapped over the knuckles for peering into a cupboard
she had no right to open. His look and his tone of
voice said clearly: 'Keep out of what is private to me.'

He extended a hand in order to open the door, but
before he could turn the handle the door was thrust
open and a woman came hurrying out, colour high on
her cheekbones.

'Ah, *signore*,' she gestured into the room, 'that one in
there lies staring at the wall and refuses to be washed.
She has taken no nourishment the entire day and has
just informed me that if she can drag herself to the
balcony she is going to throw herself to the courtyard.
I was about to fetch Antonio——'

'There is no need for that, Malina.' The Don indicated Dominique with a curt movement of his hand.
'This young woman is the sister of the *signora* and she
may be able to deal with the present upset. May I ask
what induced it?'

The woman flicked eyes over Dominique. 'She
has developed a rash, *signore*, no doubt from the barbiturates. She needs them so she can sleep, but such
things are good for no one. Drugs! Poison!'

Dominique couldn't take her eyes from this woman
whom the Don had called Malina. She had been ex-

pecting someone a lot older, but the Italian woman—
the nanny who had rescued Tony—looked about forty
and her looks were striking. There wasn't a thread of
grey in her sleek black hair worn in a bun, her gaze
was sharp and dark, and her features were chiselled
and regular, with a velvety mole high on her cheek-
bone, just beneath her left eye. Her eyes were in-
credibly dark, pupil and iris merging.

Not only did Dominique feel surprised, she felt an
instant stab of resentment at the way Malina referred
to Candice, speaking to the Don as if Tony's wife was
the servant. Dominique's natural concern for her sister
increased all the more, while her opinion of Don
Presidio sank a notch lower. That he should place
Candice in the hands of this basilisk-eyed woman sent
a chill through her blood. Candice, who had loved
sunshine and gaiety and the admiring affection of
people. Even the busy Sisters of Saint Anselma had
made that extra bit of fuss of her because she had been
so bright-minded and vital.

Dominique shivered . . . Candice of all people talking of suicide!

'It sounds as if I've arrived here just in time.'
Dominique spoke in cool tones but couldn't quite keep
a smouldering anger out of her eyes. 'My sister obviously needs me, not only as a nurse but as someone
who cares about her. May I go in to her?'

The Don inclined his head.

'May I go alone?' Dominique hung on to her dignity
and strove not to give Malina a look that would have
expressed her aversion. From now on that woman
would be kept out of Candy's room; she would insist
on it.

'If that is your wish?' The Don met her eyes briefly,
then he opened the door of her sister's room and with

a murmur of thanks she walked past him and Malina, closing the door firmly behind her.

She stood just inside the room a moment, feeling the nervous beat of her heart, then calling upon her compsure she crossed to the bedside and saw Candice lying still in a tangle of ivory silk sheets, her face to the wall, her pale gold hair tangled on the pillows.

Dominique took her sister by the shoulders and felt instantly the resistance in the frail figure. 'Candy, do turn over so I can give you a hug and a kiss,' she murmured.

For several seconds there was no response from Candice, then a sob shuddered its way through her body. 'Nicky—you?'

'Yes, my dear.' With tender concern and expertise Dominique turned Candice to face her, feeling a shock when she saw how thin and pallid was the face which she had last seen glowing in a frame of furs. The gold hair was lustreless and the pale lips were dry-looking, and one side of the wasted face was marred by a rash . . . the rash which Malina attributed to the drugs which Candice took in order to sleep.

Dominique kissed her sister gently, but the blue eyes remained bleak and almost hostile. 'Aren't you pleased to see me?' she asked.

'Why should you bother about me—you had other people to take care of, didn't you?'

'Had I known about all this, Candy, I would have come a lot sooner,' Dominique assured her. 'I'm sure Tony wanted to let me know, but it seems that his brother is in charge and expects everyone to bow to his commands. I received his Telex yesterday and was given immediate leave to come and take care of you. The Don tells me that you've been in the hands of a very good doctor and that——'

'That I lie here like a log because I enjoy it?' Candice broke in wildly. 'I can't walk, Nicky! As God is my witness I've tried—how I've tried, but I fall down in a heap and then I start to cry a-and that upsets Tony. Oh, what am I going to do?'

Candice clung to Dominique so fiercely that her fingernails stabbed through the material of her suit. 'You've got to help me before I lose my reason—that and Tony! I love him so, a-and there's someone else——'

'Hush!' Dominique stroked the tangled hair off the hot brow and her own distress almost matched her sister's. 'You must stop believing such lies about him——'

'They aren't lies.' Candice said it tonelessly. 'I saw guilt in his eyes when I accused him. You know when you see that, like a veil I wanted to rip away from his face. I—I think I could almost have forgiven him had he told me the truth, but he lied—he lied, and bought me those horrid pearls as a cover-up! Did Presidio tell you about the pearls?'

'Yes, he told me.' Dominique sat down on the side of the bed and eased the listless head against her shoulder. 'He said you struck Tony with them, he raised his hand to you and taking fright you fell down some stone steps. He said you were only bruised and a trifle concussed at the time, and that this inability to walk came on later. Candy, it could be psychosomatic, and if that's the case it's up to your mind to do the healing——'

'You all talk as if I'm going mad,' Candice sobbed. 'I've seen the way Tony looks at me—am I crazy? Is that what's wrong with me?'

'Of course you aren't crazy.' Dominique managed a smile, but she was deeply troubled by her sister's altered appearance and loss of vitality. Despite the Don's assurance that his brother had not betrayed Candice with another woman, Dominique was becoming convinced that he had done something to bring about this drastic change in a girl who had been aglow with life. Her sister's hurt and pain went so deep that her very nerve centre was involved.

As a nurse Dominique had seen what a nervous breakdown could do to people. No one was immune from such a breakdown and when it happened it took all the spirit out of the afflicted person. Dominique faced the fact that her task was going to be far from easy; it was up to her to put the fight back into Candice: the will to live and laugh again. It was shocking to see her so dispirited and so deprived of all the pride she had taken in her looks.

'Your hair's looking a mess,' she commented, willing herself to speak in a teasing voice. 'Tomorrow I'll give it a good shampoo and set, would you like that?'

'Why bother?' There was a bitter twist to Candy's lips. 'Tony isn't interested any more in how I look. Everything he ever said, everything we ever enjoyed together has been a lie. He told me I was beautiful, but all the time he was thinking of someone else.'

'That's nonsense,' Dominique said briskly. 'He wouldn't have married you if he cared for someone else.'

'He married me because I—I told him a lie.'

'What do you mean, Candy?'

'Don't tell me you're that innocent!' The twist of bitterness made Candice look almost ugly for a moment. 'Tony and I spent a weekend in Paris. Every moment was marvellous, but I knew he had no intention of marrying me. I bided my time and then pretended I was going to have his child—he's very Latin and chivalrous, and I wanted him at any cost. It was easy enough after we were married to say I'd been mistaken—perhaps that's why he hates me.'

'Candice!'

'Lies beget lies, don't they, Nicky? Our sins have a way of finding us out.' A tear trickled forlornly down Candy's thin cheek. 'I was so—vain! It just didn't occur to me that Tony might have someone here in Italy whom he cared for—an Italian girl who wouldn't go off to Paris with him and then con him into a marriage. I deserve what's happened to me! I've earned it and now I'm paying the price!'

'You mustn't talk this way.' Dominique gathered her sister close to her, stroking the tangled hair and rocking her as if she were still the little sister who sometimes cried in the night when they were sent to the convent and missed their father. 'Whatever Tony believed when he married you, I know what I sensed when I saw you together at Christmas time. He does care about you, my dear, and you must believe it and build on it and things will come right for you. You knew you weren't marrying a cosy, average sort of man when you chose to love Tony Romanos. He and his brother aren't exactly run of the mill, are they?'

Candice sighed deeply and lay looking at Dominique with sad eyes. 'What do you think of Presidio? Some people find him arrogant; other say that since the death of his girl he's become a misogynist.'

'She must have been very young when she died.' Dominique's gaze was upon her sister's left hand; her rings were loose and her fingernails were in need of a manicure. It was so unlike Candy to neglect herself.

'Yes, she was young,' Candice said in a resigned sort of voice. 'It seems to run in the family, doesn't it?'

'I don't quite——' Dominique's fingers clenched her sister's.

'I'm twenty-three, Nicky. That isn't old, is it?'

'I'm not going to listen to such talk—you aren't dying!'

'My legs are dead.'

'You only mean that they feel dead.'

'Isn't it the same? I can't walk on them, and I certainly can't dance any more. Tony loves to dance. We talked about opening a dancing school, but he didn't think his brother would approve.'

'Did he ever mention the idea to Don Presidio?' asked Dominique.

'No, we just used to mull it over and felt that we could make a go of it if he could persuade Presidio to advance the money for the initial outlay. Tony has some money of his own and Presidio makes him an allowance based on the income of the estate, but we'd need capital in order—anyway, when those foul letters arrived it was as if—as if the bottom dropped out of the world. I didn't want to believe the things in them, Nicky, but they were so mocking and knowing! I burned the first letter—I just couldn't bring myself to show it to anyone! Then another one came and I happened to open it just as Presidio was coming out of his office. He saw how upset I was and insisted on reading the thing. He said I was foolish to believe such a pack of lies, but there was a reference in it to a scar high up on Tony's thigh, and it was put so salaciously——'

Sudden colour washed away the pallor from Candy's face. 'Can you blame me, Nicky, for being suspicious? I tackled Tony and he made denials, but there was something in his manner that rang false, and then he bought those pearls a-and I almost hated him for it, as if—as if he was trying to buy me off. Men are such brutes at times!'

'Are they?' For just a while longer Dominique wrapped her arms about Candice and treated her like a small hurt child, but soon she was going to have to be tough with her. Her spirit had to be aroused. Her pride in herself had to be reawakened. She had to be pulled out of the womb of despair into which she had crawled.

'I—I used to think you were a fool to want to become a nun,' Candice murmured. 'Now I begin to think that you're better off without a man in your life.'

'Possibly so.' Dominique stroked the lank hair out of her sister's eyes. 'How would it be if I made you nice and tidy before your evening meal? Just look at this nightie, all grubby around the yoke, and your hair looks like a wild pony's mane. I hear that you've managed to scare away your other nurses, but I'm staying the course. You can't frighten me away.'

'I suppose he met you off the steamer?' asked Candice.

'He did.'

'How magnanimous of him! I suppose he wanted to paint me black so dear Tony would come out like the white knight? He didn't want me here in the first place; it's common knowledge that he doesn't intend to marry, so it rests with Tony to supply the heir to all the Romanos holdings. The almighty Don Presidio would have liked that heir to be as Italian as Tony and himself, now it looks as if there won't be even a half-Latin heir to the estate.'

'You mustn't think like that or talk like it,' Dominique reproved. 'From now on your attitude is going to be a fighting one——'

'*Onward, Christian Soldiers* and all that?' Candice mocked.

'Yes, we'll even sing it together if it will help.'

'You're priceless, Nicky, you always were. But I—I haven't got your faith in human nature.'

'You've got to have faith in yourself, Candy. We're going to fight this battle together and I shall insist on exercises so your legs will keep pliable, then we'll go swimming——'

'Tony hates the sea!'

'We're talking about you.' Dominique gripped the thin nervy hands. 'All I'm concerned about is getting you well, and when that's accomplished the world will look a different place to you—you'll see. Have you your own bathroom?'

Candice indicated a door at the far end of the room and Dominique went to take a look. As she had hoped, the bath was a deep one in the Roman style, square and black-tiled. 'Good,' she said. 'I'm going to teach you leg exercises while you're in the bath and when you start to feel confident we'll go and try your legs in the sea—and don't pull that face!'

'You're clucking like a mother hen,' Candice grumbled.

'I'm talking sense. You want to get back on your feet, don't you?'

'Do I?' Candice looked moody and her gaze strayed to where the balcony loomed beyond the windows, reminding Dominique of what Malina had said to the Don, that Candice had threatened to crawl out on the balcony and throw herself over.

'What time do you have your evening meal?' Dominique went to the dressing-table and found a hairbrush, silver-backed and initialled CJR, her sister's middle name being June. Her own middle name was May, a charming idea of their father's, a man whom Candice probably took after; a man capable of evading his responsibilities. In a sense her sister was trying to escape, having convinced herself that Tony desired only her body and not her heart. The body she had used in order to make him marry her. The body which had plunged down stone steps and lain at his feet bruised and sprawled.

'I have my dinner about half-past seven.' Candice submitted to the hairbrush, wincing as Dominique dealt with the tangles.

'Does Tony join you?'

'Sometimes, when he has nothing better to do—ouch, that hurts!'

'You shouldn't let your hair get all snarled up. From the look of this mop I shouldn't think you've touched it with a brush or comb for days. I can remember your hair looking like a shining cape around your shoulders; you used to spend hours on your appearance.'

'Why should I bother now?' Candice spoke sullenly. 'I'm not going anywhere.'

'Do you never leave this room? Doesn't Tony ever take you out for a drive?'

'I prefer to stay here.'

'What nonsense! You can't shut yourself away in a stuffy bedroom; you need sunshine and fresh air.'

'Is that why you came here, Nicky, so you could nag me? I get enough nagging from Presidio—he had a damned wheelchair delivered to the villa, but I refused to be lifted into it. He tried to force me—arrogant brute!'

'A wheelchair sounds like a good idea,' Dominique said.

'He'd really like to put me away in a home—Malina told me. Have you met her?'

'Yes.' Dominique drew the hair brush slowly down the untangled gold hair. 'I understand that she's very attached to Tony and was once his nanny. A nanny usually leaves a household when her charge starts to grow up.'

'Not Malina!' Candice said with feeling. 'She wormed her way right into the family and the time never came for her to leave—it all goes back to when Tony lost his parents and she saved him. Both Presidio and Tony felt they owned her a debt of gratitude and she wangled a permanent home out of them. You may have noticed that she doesn't behave like a servant.'

'Yes,' Dominique said quietly, 'I noticed.'

'You didn't like her, did you, Nicky?'

'Not particularly.'

'Did she have something to say about me?'

'She said you made a threat—about throwing yourself over the balcony.'

'Lying old moo!' exclaimed Candice.

'Didn't you make such a threat, Candy?'

'As if I would?'

Dominique didn't know what to think, and then her thoughts were scattered as the door opened and Don Presidio stepped into the room. Very tall and dark, he came to the foot of the bed and gazed very deliberately at the two sisters.

'What do you want?' Candice asked, on the edge of rudeness.

'To ask how you like your surprise.'

'Nicky being here, do you mean?'

'You are pleased to have her here?'

'Delirious!' Candice drawled.

'Your impudence, Candice, makes me want to spank you.' His eyes held a dangerous gleam. 'Are you going to treat your sister the way you have treated your other nurses? She knows of your childish tantrums.'

'How would you behave if you lost the use of your

legs?' Candice gazed back at him sullenly. 'Anyway, you kept Nicky away from me for weeks—you and Tony!'

'Your sister has her way of life, and you had excellent nurses whom you chose to insult with your churlish behaviour. I hope you will now mend your ways—I notice that she has managed to make you look a little less dishevelled.' He glanced at Dominique. 'I congratulate you, *signorina*.'

She gave him a steady look, seeing in him a steely charm which didn't quite convince her that he was a misogynist. 'May I ask you something, *signore*?'

'Please proceed.'

'I wish to be in sole charge of my sister and I would like it understood that no one else is to enter this room with the intention of giving orders and upsetting her.'

'I see. Have you anyone particular in mind?'

'The woman to whom you introduced me a short while ago.'

'Malina?'

'Yes.' Dominique looked at him with a quiet air of dignity. 'I didn't like the way she spoke, as if Candice were a petulant child with a pretence ailment. I am the nurse, not Malina. I know my own sister better than any of you. I can assure you that Candy's sickness is genuine, added to which she is your sister-in-law and entitled to respect. I saw very little of it in that woman's manner.'

'I warned you of her tendency to speak her mind,' he rejoined.

'There is a difference, *signore*, in speaking one's mind and being contemptuous.'

'Yes,' he agreed. 'Right now you are speaking your mind, eh?'

'I speak my mind when I feel I'm in the right.'

'It would seem so.' He regarded Dominique with an eyebrow at a sardonic angle. 'Have you any more requests to make?'

'I daresay I shall think of a few. For instance, in a few days' time I shall want to take Candy down to the beach. Is there someone who can carry her down?'

'*Si.*' He gave that brief, almost courtly bow. 'Myself.'

Her eyes skimmed the breadth of his shoulders. '*Grazie*—it will do my sister all the good in the world to swim in the sea. In my hands she's going to take exercise, not be allowed to lie in bed the whole day so that when night falls she has to take a drug in order to sleep.'

'You sound something of a martinet, but a sensible one,' he commented.

'I hope I am.'

'You didn't imagine, Presidio,' Candice gave an off-key laugh, 'that Nicky was demure, with her eyes cast down? She might look as if butter wouldn't melt in her mouth, but she has her share of the Davis temperament. She's no angel.'

'Is that so, *signorina*?' His gaze was disconcertingly direct, but Dominique didn't evade it. No doubt he was used to making women feel selfconscious, but she had no right to feel conscious of herself where a man was concerned.

'Heaven is the place for angels,' she said, 'and I'm all too aware of being human. What's for dinner, I wonder? I didn't feel like eating lunch on the steamer and now I'm ravenous.'

'I did hear mention of *cannelloni*.' His eyes were amused. 'It's a delicious Italian dish, far removed from the mortifying of the flesh.'

'I'm sure I shall enjoy every bite, *signore*.'

'Ah, so you don't live on bread and water?'

'Only on Fridays,' she murmured, 'with a pinch of salt.'

'Or a pinch of pepper,' he drawled.

'Sister Paprika!' Candice laughed in her high-strung way. 'You'll have to call yourself that when you become a nun, Nicky. Did you know, Presidio, that my sister is to become a holy vessel from which no man may quench his thirst?'

'Yes, I had been informed of the pending event.' He glanced at Dominique, catching her gaze before she could look away. 'It moved me to remark how unalike a pair of sisters can be.'

'That goes for brothers as well,' Candice murmured.

'It does indeed, *carina*.' Abruptly his face was stern. 'Well, Miss Davis, you may count yourself as the sixth nurse to enter this house. May I ask if you feel confident about the task you are taking on?'

'Yes,' she said quietly. 'If I have your assurance that I'm in control of this sickroom, apart from the doctor, of course.'

'Of course,' he echoed. 'Get some sense into the candy-floss head of this sister of yours and I'll buy you a gold watch. Is that a bargain?'

Dominique flushed, but not with pleasure. 'I have a watch, *signore*,' she showed him her wrist and the nickle-silver dial on a thin leather strap. 'It will be reward enough for me if Candy gets well. I don't accept presents.'

'Is it forbidden?' he mocked.

'Yes, by me,' she rejoined.

CHAPTER THREE

THE stars hung low enough to be plucked out of the sky, or so it seemed, and the air was soft, fragrant, almost heady. If Dominique listened carefully she could hear the waves lapping the rocks far down on the beach.

So rarely had her life held moments like this, and she took pleasure in such peace and beauty, when she could come out on the *terrazza* and feel the enchantment of the night seeping into her very bones and helping her to relax.

Most of her daytime hours were spent with Candice, whose moods were still uncertain; whose response to Dominique's régime had its ups and downs. With a mixture of temper and sulkiness she allowed her legs to be exercised. She was eating better, but because she was being weaned off the barbiturates her sleep was fitful and she was restless at night. Dominique would read to her, or they would chat about their convent upbringing and the Sisters whom they had liked.

Dominique tried to conceal the deep concern she felt for Candice, for her sister was far from well and so altered in her ways. The look in her eyes was so often desperate that it haunted Dominique. She felt sure there was something Candice was holding back, something she wouldn't—or couldn't—talk about, and it seemed to be eating the heart out of her.

A sigh caught in Dominique's throat. She couldn't force Candice to tell her what was causing her such despair; she could only hope that one sleepless night her sister would be driven to confide in her. It wasn't until she let that happen—like letting poison out of a wound—that she would start to heal, and Dominique knew it.

She let her gaze rove among the stars, sparkling points of silver in the velvety darkness of the Italian sky. Life for Candice in such a place should have been romantic and filled with happiness . . . it was like Eden, and again Dominique wondered if there was a serpent in the garden, who had directed its venom at her sister, made so vulnerable by her love for Tony. The thought stirred anger through her and almost spoiled the beauty of the night. There had to be an author of those cruel letters, and there was a possibility that their author resided in this house.

A name stole in and out of Dominique's mind, but without evidence, and because charity was part of her nature, she resisted the impulse to confront the owner of that name with her suspicions. She could be mistaken and she certainly didn't wish to cause an upset which might result in her dismissal from the villa.

Candice needed her . . . badly.

When she returned to her sister's room she found Tony there and was pleasantly surprised. His visits to his wife weren't all that frequent, perhaps because he couldn't bear to see how changed Candice was from the lively, affectionate girl she had been. Nowadays she would either be listless or she would start an argument with him which ended with her in tears or with Tony slamming out of the room.

Tonight a single look told Dominique that her sister was in one of her withdrawn moods. She lay on the *chaise-lounge* in the flattering glow of a ruby-shaded lamp, wearing a lace and satin negligee, her legs covered by a lace throwover, a lovely handmade article which had taken on an ivory hue with age. Candy's hair was brushed and combed so that it framed her pale face like gold silk. Her appearance and that of the room were pristine by comparison to how they had been upon Dominique's arrival, and she saw the appreciation of this in Tony's eyes when he arose from his armchair and smiled at her.

He was tall like his brother, lean and animal-graceful, but iron charm didn't enclose Tony like armour. He had a less Romanesque nose and chin, and his taste in clothing was rather more flamboyant. Tonight he wore a dinner jacket lined with grey silk to match his silk corded shirt. There was the gleam of a gold watch at his wrist and another gleam of gold at his cuffs. His crisp black hair was perfectly groomed and he certainly had a very romantic aura.

Dominique could understand her sister's infatuation for him; to all outward appearances he was the epitome of Latin courtesy and charisma. But she couldn't help but wonder what secrets might lie behind those handsome dark eyes ... eyes without that strange silvery effect which locked the Don away with his memories.

'Nicky, you are achieving miracles,' he said enthusiastically. 'Candy looks so much better these days and it's all due to you. You have the *pazienza* of a saint!'

'I assure you I'm no saint,' she smiled. 'Candice is taking a more positive view of herself and she wants to get well, don't you, *carina*?'

Candice didn't answer, she just lay there and gazed blankly in front of her, though Dominique suspected that she was gazing upon some mental screen and seeing there the tall, good-looking image of Tony with his arms around another woman ... a woman who knew him as intimately as Candy did herself.

Dominique studied her sister, the golden hair spilling around her heart-shaped face, the hollows of her cheeks filled with ruby shadow cast by the lamp on the table beside the lounger.

'What do you fancy for dinner tonight?' Dominique asked.

'I'm not hungry,' Candice sighed. 'I'll just have a glass of champagne.'

'I've been talking to Cook,' Dominique fingered the lace of the throwover. 'She's baking veal and prawns and they're enormous, the size of crabs. Doesn't the thought make your mouth water?'

'Not particularly.' Candice gave a delicate yawn. 'I'll have a few cream crackers with the champagne.'

'Really, *cara*,' Tony gave a slightly impatient laugh, 'you can't insult Moët et Chandon with a few cream crackers!'

'Then make it caviar,' she drawled.

'Come along,' Dominique was determined that these two wouldn't argue tonight, 'that baking veal smelled delicious, and you can have asparagus served with it. Don't be moody, dear. Think of all the girls who would like to live in a house like this one, with a handsome husband. Count your blessings!'

'I do, Nicky.' A sharp note had come into Candy's voice. 'I really do think it's wonderful having to lie here like this when I—I'd like to be out dancing and having a good time. This should have happened to you and then you'd be able to call yourself a real martyr!'

'Candice!' The name broke shocked from Tony's lips. 'What a way to speak to your sister! Your tongue should catch on fire!'

'It's a pity you didn't!' she said venomously.

He went ashen beneath his tanned skin and Dominique felt a stab of pity for the pair of them, torn apart as the writer of those poisonous letters had hoped they would be. Was it possible there was another woman in Tony's life, and was it she who had wielded a pen which had struck sharper than a knife?

'I'm getting out of here!' Tony made for the door.

'Tony—don't!'

He paused, a hand stretched to open the door, then something in that wailing cry made him turn and come slowly back to the side of the lounger. He gazed down sombrely at Candy's stricken face, at her hands reaching out to him.

'You say viperish things to me,' he growled.

'I don't mean to——'

'You say them as if you mean them.'

'I—it's because I'm so frightened. Hold me, Tony! Hold me and stop me from thinking!'

He knelt quickly on the rug and gathered the slight figure into his arms. Dominique watched and prayed silently that Candy's contrition wasn't a momentary thing. The thin arms stole about Tony's neck and he kissed the pleading lips.

Candy sighed and buried her cheek against his coat, and Tony turned to look at Dominique. He quirked an eyebrow as if to ask her what he was going to do with his wife, a shrew one moment, and a little girl lost the next.

'We'll have dinner together,' he said. 'Tell them down in the kitchen to send up the full menu and I'll try to get Candy to eat. We'll have champagne to go with it, but no cream crackers.'

Dominique smiled slightly. Did he love her sister, or did he feel duty bound to act as if he did? Was there a look of pain in his eyes or a shadow of hurt or guilt? If only one or the other of them would confide fully in her ... without that kind of co-operation she was like someone swimming against a treacherous tide, even as she made progress she was swept back again into the lash and sting of the waves that swept Tony and Candice in and out of each other's arms.

'Tell me everything,' she wanted to say. 'Let me be your confessional!'

'I'll go and see about your dinner,' she said gently, and left them as they were, quiet in each other's embrace for a while.

Dominique was coming through the green baize door that led from the kitchen into the hall when the Don himself appeared from his cellar carrying a long-necked bottle with that certain air that indicated a wine of significance. He was clad in his severely dark dinner-suit (sable, like a suit of armour) and as she prepared to pass him with a polite nod of the head, he spoke to her.

'Nurse, are you planning to dine alone?'

The brilliant hall lights reflected on her glasses as she gave him a startled look. 'Yes, *signore*. Your brother is with Candice.'

'I thought so. You will take dinner with me tonight.' He said it rather imperiously. 'You have no objection?'

'You know my objection, Don Presidio.' She gazed at him with a certain gravity which belied an inward lack of calm. 'It is best that I keep to myself and remain just the nurse in your house. You did promise——'

'No, *signorina*, I merely bowed to your wish at the time, and I see no reason why you should dine off a tray tonight when I am about to open a bottle of my favourite wine.' He stroked a hand down the bottle, almost sensuously. 'The Tears of Tiberius—you have heard of him?'

'He was a Roman tyrant,' she said, a little shake of emotion in her voice. She wasn't quite sure if she was angry with him for brushing aside her wishes, or afraid of being alone in his disturbing company.

The Don's firm lips gave a twitch. 'You do take wine, don't you? It isn't among the pleasures you've forsworn?'

'I—I think it best that I eat in my room——' She started towards the stairs, but was curtly ordered to remain where she was.

'When I give a order in my house I expect it to be obeyed,' he said.

'You are ordering me to—to dine with you, *signore*?'

'I am, *signorina*.'

'But I'm still in my uniform.'

'So I notice.' His eyes flicked over her as if he might be wondering what she looked like in an evening dress. 'I can allow you half an hour in which to change. Is thirty minutes sufficient?'

'Yes, but I don't think——'

'No, just don't think,' he said drily. 'You do a little too much of it and it isn't good for you. Now and again you should allow yourself the freedom to be thoughtless—like other women.'

'I—I'm not like other women——'

'Nonsense!'

'You know what I mean, *signore*.' She felt herself flushing under his gaze and was torn between making a dash for the stairs and remaining here to get the better of this debate—the man was altogether too fond of his own way!

'Miss Davis,' he said, 'don't be so damned prim and proper. I'm sure even the good Sisters of Saint Anselma enjoy the occasional glass of wine with their supper. The Almighty wouldn't have given us the vines if we weren't meant to enjoy the grapes. Is that not logical, even to a rather illogical English nurse who has decided, for some forsaken reason, that she isn't the sort of company a man should keep?'

'You only want to amuse yourself,' she said defensively. 'I've been told that you haven't a great deal of time for women.'

'It's true,' he agreed blandly. 'I haven't much time for a great deal of women, but you're hardly that, are you? Do you fast?'

'I beg your pardon?'

'Or is it all that running up and down stairs that does it?'

'Oh——' she glanced down at herself, 'I see what you mean. I've always been rather skinny, but it helps, being a nurse.'

'Even when it comes to lifting patients a couple of sizes larger than yourself?'

'There's a knack to it, *signore*.'

'You mean you could lift me if I were in your hands?'

Of themselves her eyes skimmed his height and breadth. He gave an illusion of leanness, but more than once she had noticed the muscularity of his shoulders, especially when he came in from riding and was wearing one of his polo-necked jerseys.

'You look far too fit to ever fall into my hands,' she rejoined, when he quirked a brow at the way she scanned him.

He smiled briefly, then gestured with a lean hand towards the stairs. 'Go and change into a dinner dress. The Tears of Tiberius will wait a while.'

'I haven't such a dress.' She could feel the heat in her cheeks and pushed nervously at the frame of her spectacles . . . the admission somehow made her feel like Little Orphan Annie.

'Then borrow one of your sister's,' he said in exasperation. 'I'm sure she has dozens of them.'

'I couldn't——'

'Nurse, you are beginning to make me lose my temper.' His eyes glittered. 'You are trying to evade my invitation, but you aren't getting away with it—wear a shirt and a skirt, but for heaven's sake get yourself out of that uniform for an hour. And that's very definitely an order!'

'Very well, *signore*,' she backed towards the stairs. 'I'll see you in the dining-room in half an hour.'

'You will see me out on the *corte mortella*,' he rejoined. 'It's a fine night, so a table has been set for dinner outside. Have you any objection to make about that?'

'No——'

'Your eyes said something else, Nurse.' He looked at his most sardonic. 'Don't imagine that those glasses hide you from people—do you need to wear them all the time?'

'Yes, I'm blind as a bat without them.'

'Haven't you ever thought of trying contact lenses?'

'No, why should I?'

'Vanity is a good reason, for most women.'

'I—I don't happen to be vain.'

'Don't you?' he mocked. 'One of the requisites for the devout life?'

'I'd rather not talk about what is private to me, if you don't mind, *signore*.'

'What a pity,' he drawled.

'You don't like to talk about what is private to you,' she defended herself, wishing to goodness she had lingered a few more minutes in the kitchen, then she would have avoided this confrontation which had led to an invitation she didn't want. She was alarmed by the very thought of dining with the Don out on the myrtle court, one of the most attractive areas of the garden.

'Would you like to be my confidante?' he asked.

'No—indeed not!'

'No?' His eyebrow and the edge of his lip quirked in unison. 'I had the distinct feeling you felt curious about my private life.'

'As if I would be?'

'You'd be a strange sort of female if you lacked curiosity about people, especially those of the masculine gender. Come, Miss Davis, you aren't locked into your chastity belt just yet.'

'Y-you find me something of a joke, don't you, Don Presidio?'

'I find you something of a mystery,' he amended.

Dominique stood there feeling the nervous beat of her heart. 'Why am I such a mystery to you?' she demanded. 'Haven't you forsworn marriage just as I have?'

'Yes.' A dangerous little flame came to life in his eyes, smouldering there in their darkness. 'Go and change into something a little more frivolous. I shall be waiting for you with the wine.'

She ran upstairs, pursued by the look which her words had brought into his eyes. She knew she had probed a deep-seated nerve in the man, jabbing through the ice in which it was kept numbed. Heaven help her, she had wanted to keep him at a distance, but they had both said things which strangers didn't say to each other, and quite desperately she wanted an excuse not to dine alone with him.

When she looked in upon Candice, however, her sister and Tony seemed content with each other's company there in the warm glow of the lamplight. 'Everything all right?' she asked.

'Fine,' Tony assured her. 'You run along and have your own dinner.'

She smiled, but it faded when she entered her room and took a look at what hung in her wardrobe. She decided that the dove-grey skirt of her suit and a white shirt with some pin-tucks would have to satisfy the Don's demand for something frivolous. Dressed and neat, with her hair coiled into its nape knot, she had an air of composure that was deceptive. She made her way out to the *corte mortelle* upon very reluctant legs, walking among walls upon which half-wild roses were tangled.

The table was set for two beneath the boughs of the myrtle trees; there was a glint of silver, the sheen of crystal, and the sound of water trickling into the basins of a fountain. *Cigales* could be heard but not seen among the scented cypress trees, a scent that mingled duskily with that of the dark-red roses, the camphor flowers and the magnolias. Within a little stone grotto fish slipped among the shining lily leaves like slithers of gold, and the scene was lit by lanterns in scrolled iron sconces attached to the walls of the small courtyard.

The setting was so romantic that Dominique almost turned and ran away in a kind of panic ... what was she doing here among the flowers of an Italian garden, alone with a man?

'Ah, there you are, *signorina*.' He stepped out from the shadow of the trees into the lantern light that revealed the bold cast of his features and the crisp blackness of his hair. Lean and dark, she thought, and such men are dangerous!

She felt his eyes take her in from her neat unglamorous hairstyle down to her neat T-barred shoes. '*Santo Dio*,' he growled, 'You still manage to look like a nurse!'

'I am a nurse, *signore*. If you want glamorous company, then you shouldn't invite me to dine with you.'

'I invite you because it suits me to do so.' He shrugged in a very Latin way. 'You lack glamour because it suits you to be that way.'

'I lack it because I don't possess it, *signore*.' A smile quivered on her lips. 'It also takes time and money, and I have more important things to do with my time.'

'And nursing is not highly paid, eh?'

'The rewards are not in lucre,' she agreed.

'What are the rewards, you most unusual child?'

'I'm not a child,' she protested.

'Permit me to say that in some ways you are—what are the rewards, when a lot of people are so lacking in gratitude?'

'There's great satisfaction in seeing someone get well; in seeing the pallor of illness fade from their face to be replaced by a tint of colour, the dullness gone from their eyes as they start to take an interest in life again. The reward is doubly precious when a child is involved.'

'You have worked with children?' There was a quick note of interest in his deep voice.

'Yes, *signore*, at a special unit soon after I qualified as a fully fledged nurse. It was often a sad place, for it was set up for babies deformed at their birth and not expected to live. That was why I left in the end; you get to love them because you take care of them, and then the poor mites die and I—I couldn't quite face that. It was often for the best, but it was hard, seeing them born, only to have to watch them fading away.'

'So *signorina*, your nursing experiences have been varied?'

'Yes—and you thought, *signore*, that I'd be useless dealing with my own sister.'

'We all live and learn, eh?'

'We do indeed, if we care to take the lessons to heart.'

'It seems obvious that you have taken your lessons to heart, Miss Davis.'

'I've done my best.' She glanced around the *corte*, for his eyes were so disturbingly alive in that firm featured face. 'What a very pretty part of the garden this is, especially at night. Do you dine here often?'

'When the mood is upon me.' He drew one of the cane chairs out from the table. 'Please be seated, *signorina*.'

She came and sat down, and there was no way she could ignore the dark tallness of the Don and a masculine mixture of scents such as after-shave lotion on warm skin and cigar smoke clinging to the material of his dinner-jacket. She sat down rather hurriedly and told herself that her legs had not gone weak just because a man leaned over her, his personality brushing hers like the momentary touch of a hand.

'You will take wine?' he murmured.

'Have I a choice?'

'Not really.' He held the bottle in his lean hands and popped the cork and Dominique watched as he poured the tawny wine into a pair of glasses so exquisitely cut that she felt certain they were Venetian. This outwardly hard-looking man seemed to be charmed by beauty, and Dominique found herself wondering if Amatrice had been lovely to look at. And had she dined with him here under the myrtles where against the old stone walls there was a pale glimmer of Madonna lilies and the spoked fire of zinnias? Had they shared the Tears of Tiberius in the beautiful stemmed glasses?

'Here you are,' he held out one of the glasses and she took it.

'*Grazie*.' She wondered as she looked at him if a

quiet, sad ghost watched him from the shadows where the angel trumpets of the lilies were as silent as death.

'To what shall we drink?' he asked.

'To my sister's recovery,' she replied.

'Then so be it,' he raised his glass. 'May you prevail, Nurse Davis, and may your sister soon dance again.'

The words spoken in his baritone voice were so moving to Dominique that all she could do was gaze at him across the table for what seemed an endless moment.

He tilted his glass to his lips and she did the same. What was he thinking as he looked across the table at her, a plain girl in spectacles wearing a plain white shirt, her only adornment a chrome watch on her wrist?

'What a look of gravity you give me,' he mocked. 'Wine is supposed to make a woman sparkle.'

'I'm afraid I haven't much sparkle, *signore*.'

'Only because you have never tried to have it. Have you always stood in your sister's shadow?'

'No—I do no such thing!'

'Don't you?'

'No.'

'Perhaps you aren't aware of it.'

'Candice has all the looks and it would be foolish of me to—to compete with her. Anyway, all that sort of thing never interested me. I never wanted to dance the night away.'

'You only wanted to sit it out beside sickbeds, eh? My dear girl, have you never had any fun?'

'Of course I have——'

'With a young man?'

She flushed and shook her head. 'You know that isn't what I mean. I've enjoyed myself in my own way—seeing a musical, reading a book, going for a walk, singing carols at Christmas when we go round the wards. A woman doesn't have to need the company of a man.'

'It takes a rare kind of woman to say that.'

'Do you need the company of a woman in order to enjoy life yourself, *signore*?'

'I've known that sort of company, *signorina*.'

'Of course.' Dominique lowered her gaze and in that interval of silence the Don's manservant wheeled a trolley to the table and they were served with their meal—sweet, rough-skinned melon with slices of smoked salmon, a delicious macaroni served with truffle and veal, then bell-shaped pears, the tops sliced off so they could be eaten with a small spoon.

During the course of dinner the Don spoke of surface things, but Dominique was conscious all the time that he would delve deeper again when the table was cleared and their coffee was brought to them, rich dark coffee served with little cakes garnished with delicately roasted walnuts.

'Come, sit over here.' He indicated a pair of loungers near the grotto where the goldfish flicked their web-like tails through the water. She felt her heart quicken and wanted to make an excuse to go indoors to check on Candice.

With disconcerting quickness he read her mind. 'Your sister is with her husband and perfectly all right. Come, be seated!'

Dominique obeyed him, seating herself sedately on the edge of one of the loungers.

'*Santo Dio!*' With a quick movement he swung her legs on to the lounger and with a gasp she was forced to recline against the cushions. 'What obstinacy there is in you! Now remain there, just as you are, while I bring the coffee and cakes!'

It was ridiculous, yet she didn't dare to move, accepting her coffee meekly when he returned to her side. He frowned down at her. 'For the sake of heaven relax, girl! You live on your nerves like a white fox I had when I was a boy. It had burning eyes and its fur was clear and pale as you are.'

It was the sort of remark for which Dominique had no coherent reply. It sprang, she supposed, from some well of remembrance she had somehow tapped with her own personal innocence; that which clings to children and to adults who live a life of almost spartan simplicity. It was as if she were an unruffled pool reflecting his memories of boyhood, when he had loved a white fox instead of a girl called Amatrice.

She understood and yet at the same time was confused. She wasn't used to being alone with a man and had lost the composure which was hers when she was in a sickroom, dealing with something she could cope with in a calm and efficient way.

He lowered himself to the other lounger and stretched his legs. She heard him sigh, his gaze up there among the drifts of stars. 'That fox had fur as soft as moonlight on milk,' he murmured. 'It followed me about like a puppy dog, and then one day it didn't come running when I whistled and my father told me that it had probably gone off in search of a mate and if that was so, then it would forget me and revert to the wild life. The days went by and the fox didn't return; I told no one that like a big baby I cried into my pillow for my white friend with the burning eyes . . . eyes which I had thought were devoted to me.'

His words trailed off into the scented duskiness, and then a moment later a flame lit his profile as he lit one of his dark cigars. The smoke drifted, mingling with the dusky scent of roses and cypress trees and the sabre-cut leaves of the tall eucalyptus trees.

A breeze stirred across the *corte* and it was as if ghostly fingers stroked the soft hair on the nape of Dominique's neck. A shiver ran over her skin and she felt afraid . . . afraid of something she didn't dare to think about.

'Miss Davis,' the Don spoke broodingly, 'you seem to evoke in a man the need to speak of things he usually keeps to himself.'

'Why shouldn't a boy cry because he loses his pet?' She glanced at him and saw the cigar jutting from between his teeth, a black shaft with a flame at its end.

'It was the last time I cried, *signorina*.'

'But didn't you cry for——?' She broke off, leaping back mentally from the name as if suddenly she found herself on the edge of a quicksand.

'Amatrice?' The name came from so deep in his throat that it barely made itself heard.

'Please—I didn't intend to pry——' Dominique felt a blood beat that shook her heart.

'You don't pry.' He spoke sombrely. 'You have been told about her, eh? No doubt Candice informed you that I was to have been married?'

'Yes, *signore*.'

'My fiancée came from Vicovaro, the place of lovely women, it is called. There is no doubt that she was lovely—so she appeared. You spoke once to me about the tradition of the arranged marriage in Italy and I didn't deny its existence. It does exist, *signorina*, and is usually arranged when the couple are still at school. So it was with me. It was the wish of my father that I one day become the husband of Amatrice di Cenzo, a mere infant of six when her parents and mine decided that the house of Romanos should be allied to the house of di Cenzo. My parents were dead by the time I was of age to take a wife, but I stood by their wish and proposed to Amatrice.'

A gust of cigar smoke wafted to Dominique, for he had drawn hard on the cigar, making the tip glow like an angry red eye. She felt his anger at his loss of a girl who had been lovely to look at; the girl from Vicovaro destined to be wife to no one.

'What are you thinking?' he asked. 'That my story resembles that of Dante and Beatrice?'

'No, I was just thinking that it was sad.'

'You are a sentimental creature; you think with your heart!'

'You must have been saddened—when she died.'

'Maddened, *signorina*, is the word for how I felt.'

'Yes—I see that you would be. Mad at the fates——'

'The fates!' He gave a short, harsh laugh. 'What an innocent you are, to be sure! My foolish girl, we make our own fates. As you will make yours when you become a nun. From that moment on you will follow the road that leads away from romance; your preference is to burn in the *feu sacré* of chaste love. I wonder how warming are those white flames?'

'Probably as warming as the cold comfort of your own—misogyny.'

'Ah, you've heard that I'm considered something of a misogynist? Is that how you and your sister spend the nights, discussing me?'

'As if we would——' She flushed to her earlobes. 'You must consider yourself important if you think we talk about you for hours!'

'All the same my name cropped up?'

'Yes.' Her cheeks still burned. 'In passing.'

He laughed quietly. 'Don't you ever think about the kind of love your sister feels for my brother—just in passing?'

'No——'

'It's a sin to tell a lie,' he mocked. 'If you're normal enough to listen to gossip about a man, then you are normal enough to be curious about what it feels like to be in a man's arms. I wonder what has put it into your head that you must put love out of your life—do you think of love as sin and sulphur?'

'Of course I don't.' Her gaze was caught by a shining string of fragments that was a star falling into the void. 'Oh, do look at that!'

'Don't try and evade my question, Miss Davis. I don't think you're a religious fanatic, nor do I believe you are all that pious. Do you think yourself unlovable?'

The question shook deep down in her a deep-held conviction she had never revealed to anyone. How could he have known it was there . . . and then the truth shook her, like the shock wave following upon the main tremor. He knew it because he looked at her and saw her for what she was, a plain girl in glasses, lacking the sensuous glow which awakened desire in men. Gazing back down the years, she remembered the youths who had cast loving looks at Candice, a gleam of avarice in their eyes which Candy had noticed quick as a cat on a mouse. How she had laughed, and yet how she had lapped it up, a graceful cat curling her tongue in the cream that filled her saucer.

'I think myself more useful than ornamental, *signore*.' She spoke drily. 'When Candice and I were children, other children thought I had a funny face because Candy had such a pretty one. We were the Owl and the Pussycat,'

'My dear Miss Davis!'

'I didn't mind, *signore*.' Dominique gave a little laugh. 'I had tin-rimmed glasses and this funny snub nose always buried in a book. I was so different from Candice and I realised it. She was silk ribbon and I was tape. She was buttered scone and I was bread. She was sugared almond and I—I was just a plain peanut.'

'You speak of it with humour, *signorina*, but all the same all girls like to be thought of as sugar and spice.'

'I truly didn't mind that I was an owlish little creature. Why should I? Owls look funny, but they're wise—aren't they?'

' "They say you're wondrous wise," ' he quoted. ' "But I don't think you see, though you're looking at *me*, with your large, round, shining eyes ." I knew that as a boy. I always liked the wild small creatures of the night.'

'You said you would have liked to have been a sculptor of them. Have you ever tried to do any sculpture?'

'No, but I've thought about it.'

'You should take it up, *signore*. Very often when we have a yen to do something it means that we have a talent for it.'

'As you found out with nursing?'

'Yes, I did find out that I was a good nurse. It pleased me, finding out that I could be of use.'

'Then why not keep it just like that, *signorina*?' He drew his gaze from the sky and looked directly at her. 'Why go to the extreme of becoming a nun—if you don't believe that love between a man and a woman is something profane? It isn't something you shrink from, is it?'

'It's something I don't think about——'

'Why not?'

'I——'

'You are afraid to think about it,' he insisted.

'No.'

'Yes, you are. You have grown up with the idea that in order to have love you must look like Candice. You saw teachers being indulgent towards her and the other pupils vying for her friendship. Then later on it was boys and men who hung around her like moths around a lamp. You were the silent watcher in the shadows . . . the little owl with the big, wondering eyes.'

'I—I wasn't envious of Candice,' Dominique protested. 'She was more outgoing than I and I couldn't have been like her had I tried. What on earth would I have looked like had I painted my eyes and mouth and gone out wearing dance frocks? Candice had glamour. I had none.'

'You had kindness, Miss Davis,' he said almost curtly. 'There's little enough of it about, the genuine kind, I mean, that asks nothing in return. Don't allow it to lead you astray.'

'I don't follow you, *signore*.'

'Being kind and being pious are two separate things. My first school was a Jesuit one, often the case where Latin boys are concerned, and I can assure you that the rod wasn't spared in that establishment. The monastic life can make demands that can harden the personality.'

'You're talking of self-denial, of course?' she said quietly.

'Of course.' A tinge of mockery had crept back into his voice.

'Isn't misogyny a form of self-denial?'

'You seem to be insisting that I am misogynistic.'

'It's what everyone seems to believe,' she shrugged.

'Do you believe it, Miss Davis?'

'I—I don't know you well enough, Don Presidio, to really express an opinion.'

'I am not a misogynist, but I have decided that I shan't marry. It makes us two of a kind, eh?'

'It would seem so.'

'It is so, my dear young woman. You haven't a heart of ice, but you have decided that being a wife and mother is not for you.'

'A woman, *signore*, can't become a wife and mother unless she is asked.'

'So you think that you will never be asked?'

'I'm twenty-five,' a tinge of wry humour crept into her voice, 'and I've never been kissed.'

About a minute of silence followed her words; silence between them though the *cigales* shirred away in the trees, and the wall vines rustled as the night breezes got caught among them.

'You say it with humour, *signorina*.' The words drifted into the silence almost lazily, and Dominique sensed that the Don was watching her, perhaps with curiosity, from behind his cigar smoke.

'Well, it's hardly a tragedy, *signore*,' she rejoined.

'For some it might be. For some the mysterious, ineffable realms of love are everything; the rest is a kind of death.'

'It's like that for Candice,' she agreed quietly.

'But not for you—or me?'

'Certainly not for me.' Dominique felt the ebb and flow of colour beneath her skin and was glad of the shadows, the half-light which somehow dramatised the powerful cast of the Don's features and made his shoulders seem almost threatening as he lounged there, only a couple of feet from where she rested more tensely than he.

'Are you at all curious about the techniques of—kissing?' he asked, that lazy note in his voice.

'Not any more——' She broke off and glanced confusedly at the dial of her watch. 'I—I really should be going indoors, *signore*.'

'You will go when I say you can go,' he said, not bothering this time to conceal the arrogance in his voice. 'You will answer my question—was there a time when you desired to be swept into a man's arms and kissed until you were at the mercy of only your senses and not your common sense?'

'Please,' she started to rise, 'I don't want to discuss that kind of thing.'

'If you dare leave that lounger, Miss Davis, you will discover that when I want something I refuse the denial of it. Right now I wish to search out the real person concealed inside that dutiful frame of yours. I am curious about you and you will indulge me.'

'As the arrogant lord of the manor?' She sank back on the lounger and her colour was high. 'I—I don't see that it matters what I am so long as I'm a good nurse.'

'It matters in that you are related to my brother, so why should I not ask you questions about yourself?'

'You're welcome to—to ask impersonal questions, Don Presidio. The fact that I am sister-in-law to your brother doesn't give you the right to browbeat me.'

'Is that what I'm doing?'

'You know it is! You've threatened violence if I go to see how my patient is.'

'Violence, Miss Davis?' The words seemed to purr from his throat. 'I am merely suggesting that you relax and be sociable.'

'You don't make me feel relaxed, and what you call being sociable is that I allow you to be inquisitive!'

'There is something about you, Miss Davis, which invites inquisitive feelings.'

'Inquisitorial ones! Does every woman have to be

panting for a man to want her?'

'Wasn't there a time when you felt such a wanting?'

'No——'

'You all but admitted that there was—was it when your sister used to dress in her finery to go out dancing with one of her many admirers? Did you ask yourself why they clung around her and seemed not to notice that you were alive?'

Dominique stared at him in the shadowy lantern light and his face seemed dark and cruel to her. 'Does it matter,' she swallowed a kind of pain in her throat, 'do I have to tell you what I felt?'

'Tell me.'

'I felt a kind of—of bleakness.' It was true, and she remembered it now, standing there at the door of the flat, watching as Candice ran laughing down the steps to be handed into a young man's car, or a cab that would take them into the West End for an evening of gaiety and pleasure. As the cab sped towards the bright lights Dominique knew that Candy would snuggle into the man's arms and allow him to kiss her smiling red lips. It hadn't been envy which she had felt but a kind of emptiness; with determination she had filled that in with work and a gradual rising up the scale of nursing until she qualified for her state registration.

It had no longer seemed to matter that she had always stood in the shadow of her sister's popularity. Now this man took, as it were, a knife and probed into feelings long since healed.

'I'm a plain woman, Don Presidio,' she said. 'I've come to terms with it, but of course when a girl is young it's less easy to accept.'

'That beauty is skin deep?'

'Please don't think that I was bitterly jealous of Candice.'

'I don't think any such thing.'

'Then why are you probing into me—you seem to be trying to prove that I'm a sour, embittered spinster——'

'Nothing of the sort.'

'Then what is all this about?' She gave him a bewildered look. 'I am what I seem to be, I have no secrets to expose.'

'No—it would seem not.'

'You sound disappointed, *signore*. Are you?'

'I wonder.'

'As if I'd have a lurid past for you to uncover!'

'My dear young woman, do stop talking about yourself as if you haven't an iota of attraction for the male sex! Some of the plainest women in history have had lovers great beauties couldn't attract. Cool peaks of ice sometimes conceal volcanoes, and that is a fact!'

'You aren't insinuating *that* about me?' Heat seemed to travel to the roots of her hair. 'I never even look at men!'

'So I have noticed.'

'Then how can you possibly——'

'*Santo Dio*,' he laughed to himself, 'what an innocent you are!'

'Oh—I'm going indoors, a-and don't you dare to try and stop me!' Dominique jumped to her feet and all that followed her was the low, amused sound of the Don's laughter.

Dominique experienced a strange sensation as she ran indoors . . . could it possibly be chagrin? Then she almost blundered into someone who stood gazing out towards the *corte*. 'So sorry——!'

Dark eyes with a cold sheen over them looked her up and down. Malina didn't speak but merely turned her gaze back to the *corte* where the Don remained with his amusement.

Dominique seemed to burn all over as she hastened across the hall and up the staircase. She passed her sister's room, hurrying to the door of her own bedroom. She had to get inside and compose herself before going in to see Candice. She felt all churned up and her sister might notice that she wasn't her usual cool-headed self.

She drew several steadying breaths, but still her legs felt unsteady as she crossed the room to the cheval-glass in its tall carved frame, reflecting her as Malina had seen her. Grey eyes darkened to confusion behind the frames of her spectacles, her hair less neat than usual from where her head had rested against the cushioned lounger, the lingering heat colouring the thrust of her cheekbones.

She placed her hands over her cheeks and felt the heat against her fingertips. Why on earth had she told Presidio Romanos that she had never been kissed?

Dominique stared into her own eyes, then suddenly turned away from her apprehensive face and figure. She had glimpsed in her eyes fragments of the answer and she was appalled ... mortified.

She wanted no man to kiss her ... least of all *that man*, but now, because of what she had said, he would think it and each time they met the thought would be there in his eyes ... those brooding, strangely lit eyes that remembered the lovely face of Amatrice.

Slowly she turned back to the cheval-glass and gazed at herself unsparingly. As if any man, least of all *that man*, would want to kiss her! Men liked girls who were sugar and spice; candy and cream like her sister. She had always known that and she was no longer a teenager who had ached a little in of her heart because no one loved her.

She wasn't aching now ... it was probably indigestion from too much rich food!

CHAPTER FOUR

BEING a nurse Dominique had developed a kind of extra-sensory perception where the sick were concerned.

She woke suddenly in the night, in the depth of darkness, only moments before there was a rap on her bedroom door, followed by the urgent opening of it and a stream of light outlining a tall figure in the aperture.

'What do you—what's wrong?' She raised herself in alarm and sought the switch of the bedside lamp. As it came on the tall figure was coming towards her bed, lean body enwrapped in a severe dark robe.

'You must come at once to Candice,' he said. 'She seems very ill!'

Dominique's heart gave a throb, then she flung aside the bedcovers and slid from their warmth, accepting her own robe from his hands. She thrust her feet into her slippers, then hurried with him to her sister's room. Candice had seemed perfectly all right when they had said goodnight. Tony had spent a couple of hours with her, so that when Dominique had checked her pulse and found it a little fast she had assumed that being with her husband had excited Candy.

The Candy she had left neatly tucked up in her bed, with her hair smooth on the pillow and a touch of colour in her cheeks, was not the one she found right now. Her body was arched in a rigor of pain, her hair was drenched with sweat and her face was ashen, the lips drawn away from her teeth.

'Has the doctor been called?' Dominique tried to keep the panic out of her voice. It was one of the cardinal sins for a nurse to get panicky, but this was her very own sister in acute agony, the kind that was centred in her abdomen. Such distress could be caused by a number of things, but Dominique knew that appendicitis wasn't one of them. Candice had had her appendix removed when she was eleven years old; she had hated the scar on her white skin until it had faded almost away.

Candice retched and her eyes rolled as the pain tore at her insides. 'Do something,' Tony begged of Dominique. 'Can't you give her an injection for the pain?'

'I daren't—I don't know what's causing this——' There Dominique broke off, seeing Tony in a blurred way because she had forgotten to put her spectacles on. Suddenly she was remembering a case she'd had to deal with about a year ago . . . the nursing of a young man who had been acutely poisoned by some smoked mackerel.

'Tony, did Candy eat any of those large prawns with her dinner?' she asked.

He was so shaken by what was happening to Candice that for a moment or so he couldn't reply. 'Yes—yes, I think she did. But I had several myself and I'm all right——'

'It would take only one that was off!' Dominique turned urgently to her sister and without any hesitation she pushed her fingers down Candy's throat. Candy retched again and this time she vomited into the bowl which the Don had taken from the shaking hand of the young maid who had given the alarm that the *signora* was ill.

'Hurry downstairs,' Dominique said to the girl, 'and fetch me a jug of milk and a small teapot if you can find one.'

The girl gazed at her with astonished eyes, and the Don said curtly: 'Do as the nurse says, and do it as quickly as possible.'

'*Si, signore.*' The girl fled from the room and the Don caught Dominique's gaze with his own.

'You think this is fish poisoning?' he asked.

'Possibly—I can't know for sure until the doctor arrives, but she seems to have all the symptoms——'

Dominique broke off, suddenly aware of someone in the doorway of the room. She turned, thrusting the hair from her eyes, and sensed rather than clearly saw that the person standing there was Malina.

'Antonio, what is all this?' She stepped into the room. 'Why was I not awoken so I could give assistance?'

'Because I'm here and I'm a nurse,' said Dominique, her nerves and her temper so on edge that she just didn't think about minding her tongue. 'I'm not just a children's nanny!'

'We are coping.' Don Presidio was now holding the stricken figure of Candice in his arms and rocking her, and right now it didn't seem strange that he should be doing the consoling while Candy's husband stood there at a loss. 'Malina, take my brother downstairs and make coffee for him—and tell that girl to hasten herself with the milk!'

'Milk?' Malina cast a look at Dominique. 'Of what use——?'

'Don't try and tell me my job!' Dominique's voice was shaking with anxiety and the need to do something—anything to bring relief to her sister. 'Milk can act as an antidote for poisoning and I think Candice has been poisoned—by something!'

Her words rang through the room as Candice shivered and wept in the arms of her brother-in-law, and when the maid came rushing into the room with the jug of milk and the teapot Dominique took hold of the pot and directed the girl to pour some of the milk into it. When this was done she sat down on the bed at the other side of Candice and placed the spout of the teapot between her shaking lips.

'I must make you drink this,' Dominique urged. 'It's going to help you to feel better——'

But Candice drew away shuddering. 'I feel awful—I'm dying——'

'Over my dead body!' Dominique spoke fiercely. 'Just let the milk dribble down your throat, there's a good girl.'

'I can't——' The milk dribbled out of the corner of Candy's mouth.

'Come, do as you are told.' The Don spoke firmly. 'It's for your own good, child—it will ease the pain.'

'I hurt—I do hurt,' she sobbed. 'Nicky, I-I'm s-so scared——'

'I know, darling, but try and drink this—that's right, tilt back your head and let me get it into you.' Dominique manoeuvred the teapot like a feeding cup, urging the milk down her sister's throat. She felt very little doubt about what was afflicting Candice; the sweating and the pain and the ashen tinge to her skin were too much like the symptoms she had dealt with before. This had to be some kind of poisoning, and Candice had eaten prawns with her dinner.

'Please fill the pot again,' she directed the maid, noticing briefly that Malina had left the room and that Tony had sunk forward in a chair and was staring helplessly at the bed where his wife was suffering. Though Dominique couldn't see his face clearly because of her shortsightedness she could sense that he was in despair.

'It's going to be all right,' she said bracingly. 'We have things in hand and the doctor should be here soon.'

'Why couldn't it happen to me?' he blurted. 'It would be Candy's infernal bad luck to eat something bad. Do you think that's what is causing the pain?'

'I'm fairly certain. I'd be grateful if you'd go downstairs and get some ice.'

'Ice—yes, of course.' Tony stumbled to his feet and it was something of a relief to have him gone from the room. As Dominique turned her attention back to Candice, it struck her that the Don and his brother were as unalike in their ways as she and Candy. Tony had the glamour, but Presidio Romanos had the backbone; he didn't appear to be a very compassionate person, but it was there beneath his tough exterior. With a lean brown hand he stroked Candy's hair as Dominique gently urged her to try and drink some more milk. Every now and again she retched and brought some of it back, but it was getting into her stomach and it would alleviate some of the effects of the poisoning until the doctor got there and decided how to treat her.

He arrived ten minutes later and after examining Candice he confirmed that she had eaten something contaminated. 'I shan't pump the stomach,' he decided, 'but I must give her an emetic to speed up the elimination. It will make her feel weak, of course.'

Dominique nodded and turned to Don Presidio, who was just outside the door. 'You've been awfully kind to Candy,' she said quietly. 'I do thank you.'

'I hope I would be kind to anyone in trouble.' He seemed to look directly into Dominique's hazy grey eyes, his black hair rumpled, some of it falling on to his forehead. 'I shall see to it that you now have a hot sweet cup of coffee.'

'*Signore*, could you make it a cup of tea?'

He quirked a black eyebrow. 'Tea, of course. I should have realised; it's the British panacea in time of trouble, eh?'

She smiled faintly and nodded. He strode off along the corridor, tall in his severely cut robe, cool-nerved in coping with a crisis and not in the least repelled by someone racked with sickness and diarrhoea. So different from the sardonic inquisitor he had been a few hours earlier, out on the *corte mortella*.

It was almost daylight by the time Candice was feeling a little easier; the poison had been washed out of her system and finally she lay wan and sleepy between fresh sheets, carefully washed all over by Dominique and the young maid, who was sent off yawning to get a few hours' sleep.

Dr Pasquale snapped the locks of his medical bag and beckoned Dominique to one side. 'I think the *signora* will be all right now,' he said, 'but if she should go into a relapse then contact me at once. I have to say that had it not been for you, Nurse, she might now be very much worse. You are dedicated to your work, eh?'

'And to my sister.' Dominique glanced over at the bed, where Candice lay drowsily in the aftermath of what she had been through. 'She used to be such a lively and delightful person. It isn't fair—oh, I can't help but blame her husband for much of this! He seems—weak!'

'He is not the man that his brother is,' the doctor

murmured. 'All the same, a charming person—a little too good-looking, eh?'

Dominique nodded and knew what the doctor was implying; women would always like the look of Tony Romanos and it was rather unfortunate that her sister cared so much for him; she would never be able to take in her stride the fact that he might now and then permit one of those women to lead him astray.

Candice had needed stability to offset her own butterfly nature, but instead she had mated with a man who was her duplicate rather than someone she could depend upon.

It had happened and now it had to be dealt with, but at the moment Dominique felt too worn out to even think about it. Her grey eyes were shadowed with fatigue and worry, and her back was aching from the shoulders downwards.

'Where is the young man now?' The doctor ran his professional gaze over Dominique's face.

'I sent him off to smoke a cheroot while we washed Candice and changed the bed linen,' she replied. 'He was hovering and getting underfoot.'

'Well, I shall find him and tell him that he will now come and watch beside his wife while you take some rest, Nurse. You will not be of use to the patient if you overdo things yourself. Is that understood?'

She nodded, knowing the doctor to be right. She badly needed to rest and relax, and Candice was over the worst of the fish poisoning. So long as someone sat with her in order to keep an eye on her and just be there, then Dominique could snatch a little sleep.

'Dr Pasquale?'

'Yes, Nurse?' He glanced back from the doorway, a stout man with pouched eyes and a concerned manner;

the type of family doctor that was on the wane in England.

'It was fish poisoning?'

'I would certainly say so,' he nodded. 'In her run-down state your sister would be more badly affected than a fit person. Have you known her to be affected before by shellfish?'

Dominique shook her head. 'Candice has always had a healthy appetite which nothing seemed to harm, even lunches of beefburger and chips. When we were at convent school together she caught far fewer colds than I did, and later on when she became so keen on dancing she never seemed to be tired and used to go out several nights a week to various dances. She had amazing vitality, which is why I feel so—so concerned about the way she is now. We were making a little progress, and now this has to happen——'

Tears welled into Dominique's eyes; tears she might have held back had she not been feeling so worn down. Dr Pasquale patted her shoulder in a bracing way.

'Don't lose heart, Nurse. You aren't the type of young woman to let a setback interfere with your crusade. That sister of yours is in good hands; yours and those of Don Presidio. That one is more alarming than charming, eh? He means well, take it from me.'

Dr Pasquale spoke in a significant way and Dominique realised that he had been practising in San Sabina when the Don's wife-to-be had fallen ill and died. He probably knew all the facts of the case and had seen the effect of the loss on Don Presidio.

'He's far kinder than I realised,' Dominique murmured.

'*Si*, it is deep down where the purest water runs. Nurse. Deep in the rock where the vein of gold hides itself. Don Presidio can seem a forbidding man, but there isn't a vine grower or a farmer in San Sabina who hasn't cause to be grateful to him; he has kept this region co-operative while many other landlords have insisted on the old way of things and caused disruption. Don Presidio has recognised that all men have a right to their dignity.'

'And all women?' Dominique found herself asking.

The doctor considered her through narrowed eyes. 'So as a woman you can't quite make him out, eh?'

'I'm just a nurse at the Villa Dolorita,' she rejoined. 'But it must puzzle other women that a man such as he has chosen to stay single. Most men like to share their lives, don't they?'

'Most women as well, *signorina.*'

'I don't place myself in that category, Doctor, because I plan to take the veil.'

'I see.' He drew an astonished breath. 'You somewhat surprise me.'

'Why is that?'

'Because you dealt with your sister with the naturalness of a mother.' He said it very simply, with an Italian's reverence for the very word and all it implied. 'Your mind, it is made up?'

'It has been so for some time, Doctor.'

'Ah, before you came to the Villa Dolorita!'

'Y-yes——'

'And met a man such as the Don?'

'I don't follow——'

'Don't you, *signorina?*' He touched a finger to the side of his Italian nose and his eyes held a smile. 'I think you follow me very well. The Don is quite a man; he takes the eye, eh? Not handsome like the brother Tony, but he has power, and it is power that some women prefer to the obvious charm of manner.

Power and authority combined with a surprising kindness. That side of him took you by surprise, did it not?'

'I'm continually surprised by people,' she said, evading a direct reply.

'You may be surprised by yourself, Nurse. You are now in Italy and our sun has a way of warming away the inhibitions.'

'I—I wouldn't want that to happen, Doctor.'

'And why not?'

'A plain woman guards against such things.'

When she said that, Dr Pasquale took a step towards her and gazed at her intently. 'You have, *signorina*, very beautiful eyes, and possibly a nature that matches them. Plain, *bah*! What is plain when a woman has a heart and it shows in her eyes? You tell me—no, you sway on your feet and it's time you took some rest. Don't worry about your sister. I will see to it that her husband comes to sit with her.'

He left Dominique standing there, her wide grey eyes fixed upon the spot where he had stood and said that astonishing thing about her. Not that any remark about her eyes could ever change her plans; all the same it had quickened her heart to be told that she had a redeeming feature. A slight smile touched her lips, and then she walked across to the bed and leaned close to Candice in order to study her.

Candice tiredly opened her blue eyes, feathered with shadow which almost matched that blueness.

'You're all better now,' Dominique said gently. 'Go to sleep, darling, and when you wake up—'

'Nicky, what made me so ill?'

'You ate a prawn that must have been bad.'

'Food poisoning?'

'Yes.'

Candice licked her lips. 'Can I have a drink of water?'

'Of course.' Dominique poured it fresh from the iced container and assisted her sister to sit up a little while she drank it.

'Oh, that feels good.' Candice sank back against the pillow. 'I—I seem to remember drinking gallons of milk from a—*teapot*!'

'That's right.' Dominique smoothed Candy's hair, soft as a child's and pale gold in the pale morning light. 'I poured the milk into you from the spout.'

'Ugh, you know I hate milk!'

Dominique gave a slight laugh. 'It's good medicine. You must remember that when you have children and they have a tummy upset.'

'I shall never have children, Nicky. I shall be like you in that respect.'

'You won't be like me.' Dominique clenched a hand to her side. 'You and Tony will have beautiful children.'

'No.' Candice shook her head. 'It isn't just because of the way I am—it's Tony—he doesn't want them. Before I got like this he made sure—except that one time in Paris, when I pretended afterwards that I was going to have a baby. I remember—he went so white in the face, and then when I told him that I wasn't pregnant, he was—he was so relieved. He doesn't want to be a father!'

'Candy—'

'It's true. As kind as he can be, and he was terribly kind to me last night, he's not like other Italian men who want to have a parcel of children. Oh, how would I have got through last night without you and Tony! I could feel his arms around me and I remember thinking that I'd want to die in his arms.'

'But—' Dominique broke off. It was obvious that her sister believed her husband to have been her support and comfort in the night, and she decided not to enlighten her. The Don wouldn't mind, she felt sure of that. He probably understood better than anyone that his brother Tony was less proficient in a sickroom than in a ballroom. And poor Candy had been too sick to fully realise that the warm strong arms didn't belong to the husband she had a right to lean on when she was in trouble or despair.

Dominique was more than ever convinced that her sister had married a man who was never going to be as wonderful as she wanted him to be. Be that as it may, it wasn't in Dominique to disillusion her. Let her believe the best of Tony; in that direction lay her chance of recovery from the breakdown that was essentially in the mind rather than the body. In her extremity last night Candice had moved her limbs more than once and both Dominique and the Don had noticed and exchanged glances. Candice wasn't permanently paralysed, and Dominique thanked God for it. With time and patience she'd recover, and she'd dance again.

Even as she told herself this Tony came into the room; he looked dark around the chin and his hair was tousled, as if he had been dragging his fingers through it.

'*Carina*,' he came quickly to the bedside, 'the good doctor tells me that you are much improved. Is this so?' He leaned over Candice and searched her wan face. 'Ah, still the signs of *dolore*, but you are feeling improved, *bella mia*?'

'Much improved, Tonio.' A smile faintly curved the pale lips, as if like Dominique his wife noticed that he was much more the Italian boy in his concern than the usual Latin sophisticate. 'Have you been worried for me, *caro*?'

'*Dio mio*, have I been worried!' He drew her hand to

his lips and kissed each finger. 'There were times when I couldn't stay in the room and see you suffer so—your sister, this Nicky, she has been angelic. What it is to be a nurse, eh? It takes courage,' he shot a smile at Dominique, 'and a strong stomach, I think.'

'You stayed with me through the worst of it, Tonio.' Candy's blue eyes were fixed upon his haggard but still handsome face. 'I could feel your arms holding me a-and I was so grateful.'

'My arms, *carina*, but——'

Dominique nipped his shirt-sleeved arm quite fiercely with her fingertips and when he glanced at her in astonishment, she said: 'Candy needed you, Tony, and you didn't fail her, did you—you were there to hold her and comfort her. Now she has to get plenty of sleep; you'll watch over her and see that she sleeps, won't you?'

A look of comprehension dawned in his eyes. '*Si*, Nicky, I will watch over her while you take some rest. I am thankful you were here to take care of her!'

'Yes,' Dominique studied her sister's pale face framed in the silky hair, 'I'm thankful I was here. Close your eyes, Candy. Sleep and heal, my dear.'

She left the two of them alone, hoping ardently as she closed the door that all would be well if she dared to sleep. She felt weary and yet she hesitated to go to bed. At the far end of the corridor she could see daylight breaking through the long window. She wandered towards that oblong of light and curled down into the deep windowseat that was upholstered in dark-red leather. She rested her head on the leather and closed her eyes for a few blessedly quiet moments; this eased her tired eyes, but her heart was still disquieted.

Some time during the past traumatic night there had been an atmosphere of menace in Candy's bedroom,

and now Dominique was alone with only the sound of
the birds out there in the trees she sought to pinpoint
the moment when a suspicion had struck her that her
sister's upset had something ominous about it, unre-
lated to the prawns she had eaten with her evening
meal.

As on a small screen Dominique let the night time
images roll through her mind; she saw Candice in all
her distress and Tony hunched over in a chair while
the Don cradled her sister in his arms. Then, from out
of the shadows, another figure emerged to stand gazing
across the bedroom at the stricken girl, with not the
faintest trace of sympathy on her face.

Malina!

Dominique's eyes blinked open and she gazed from
the window, seeing the garden unearthly and hazy in
the pale morning light. Oh no, it wasn't possible that
jealousy had driven Malina to that extreme . . . and yet
hardly a day went by without a newspaper story in-
volving hatred and violence towards someone. A
person read such stories and dismissed the idea that
they could ever involve them personally.

No . . . she was letting her imagination run away with
her. Dr Pasquale had said that Candice must have
eaten a contaminated prawn, and he would surely know
the difference between a case of fish poisoning and the
imbibing of something more deadly.

Yet would he know it, if he had no reason to suspect
it? Because Candy had eaten prawns with her dinner
he had assumed the obvious, just as Dominique had
done . . . until that moment when Malina had entered
the sickroom and like a poisoned dart the suspicion
had flown across the room to Dominique and found its
target in her mind. There had been something so cold
and unsurprised about the way the woman had stood

there, as if she had been expecting Candy to be taken sick.

Yes, that was what Dominique had sensed, a kind of noxious curiosity such as a bad child feels when it watches a butterfly helplessly writhing after its bright wings had been torn off.

A shudder went all through her body and she drew her robe closer about her. To whom did she confide her misgivings? To the people of this household Malina was a devoted person who had saved the life of the master's only brother. She was thought much of and allowed privileges not given to other members of the staff. She had her own suite of rooms and was supplied with an income; it was as if she was accepted as a relative by the Romanos brothers.

Despite her suspicions Dominique knew that she couldn't speak of them to Tony or Don Presidio. Her only recourse was to let Malina know that she had her under surveillance and would inform the police if the slightest sign of pain and vomiting should attack Candice again.

Oh God, it was awful to have such doubts about anyone, but deep inside herself Dominique knew that Malina was viciously jealous of Candice; that she wanted her out of this house . . . out of Tony's life one way or the other.

Dominique's instinct was to go running to Tony to beg him to get Malina out of the house, but she knew he would think her mad. He would ask Don Presidio to have *her* sent away from the Villa Dolorita, and that had to be avoided at all costs. She couldn't afford to alienate Candy's husband through Malina, for that would be playing right into the woman's hands. She had to keep a still tongue in her head where the brothers were concerned, but she had to find a way to warn Malina.

A sigh shook her lips and she was on the verge of returning to her bedroom when a tall figure rounded the bend of the corridor and came towards her. Despite the haziness of her sight when she wasn't wearing her spectacles Dominique knew who approached her, the dark, tailored robe accentuating his height, his strides long and supple . . . as a tiger walks, she found herself thinking.

She remained where she was in the windowseat, hearing the morning calls of the birds as they dipped their wings against the sky, feeling the tension in herself as the Don loomed over her and handed her a steaming cup of tea.

'Thank you.' She accepted the cup of tea gratefully. 'I was longing for that.'

'Mind, don't spill it.'

Her hand was a little unsteady and she had a feeling that the trembling of her body could be seen through her robe. The night and what she had just faced about Malina were taking their toll, but it embarrassed her that he should see her in this shaken state.

'I—I've been so concerned for Candy,' she said, taking a deep swallow of the hot sweet tea, the nectar and balm that it always is to someone who has faced a crisis. 'Ooh, that does taste good!'

A smile went across his dark face and he leaned a shoulder against the panelled wall and drew his cigar case from his pocket. 'Do you mind if I smoke one of these, Nurse?'

'N-not at all——' Her lashes blinked across the grey irises of her eyes, the pupils widely expanded.

'You are not feeling a little unwell yourself?' His fingers withdrew one of the thin dark cigars and held it halfway to his lips. 'You look extremely pale and I can see that you are shaking with nerves.'

'It's been a very worrying night, *signore*.'

'Yes.' He applied the flame of his lighter to the cigar. 'Your sister sleeps?'

'Yes, thank God!' Dominique spoke fervently. 'Tony is with her and she's very much better—weak but over the worst of the—attack.'

'It does seem a pity that she should have this set-back.' Smoke eddied from his nostrils, strong yet at the same time curiously pleasant. 'She has become so much calmer and more willing to co-operate towards her own recovery.'

Dominique took another deep gulp of tea and almost felt compelled to confide her suspicions about Malina. Through her lashes she watched him lounging against the dark oak panelling and she felt the power that emanated from him, as tangible as his cigar smoke. Dared she speak out? Would he believe such a thing of someone he had trusted and supported, or would he think that she, Candy's sister, was inclined towards hysteria?

'I spoke with Dr Pasquale,' he said. 'He seemed quite certain of the cause of your sister's attack, that it was a virulent prawn.'

Her heart thudded . . . how strange that he should make the remark, almost as if he were seeing into her mind and glimpsing a dark suspicion there.

'I——' she hesitated and he looked enquiring. 'I suppose it was.'

'What else could it have been?' he asked, and his eyelids drooped through a veil of smoke and with rumpled black hair he looked slightly younger so that a likeness to Tony was more evident.

Tony, she thought, with far less backbone than this man but Candy's husband all the same. She just couldn't risk a confrontation about Malina; she had to remain under the same roof as Candice and try to make sure in her own way that the pain and terror of last night weren't repeated.

'You look very pensive,' the Don remarked. 'Last night was almost as much of an ordeal for you as for your sister, eh?'

She nodded.

'You get very involved, don't you?' His smoke-clouded eyes were intent upon her face. 'I think you absorb other people's trouble as a blotter mops up ink.'

'I wouldn't be a very good nurse if I didn't get involved, *signore*, and Candice is my sister.'

'You cannot live her life, you know.'

'No, but I can try to save it. Don Presidio, you adopt an air of cynical hardness, but you showed a lot of concern last night.'

'Of course. To me Candice is little more than a child, and it was distressing to see her in such distress.'

Dominique gazed out at the garden where the sun had broken and was bathing its lushness in golden warmth. Gone was the night, but she couldn't seem to forget her sister's stricken eyes. Suddenly she quivered for the Don had stepped across to her and placed a hand upon her shoulder; she felt the warm hardness of his grip to her very bones.

'Go to your bed, Nurse. You've earned a good rest.'

She glanced up at him, gravity in her grey eyes. 'I— I must go and check on Candy first——'

'Tony will be vigilant of her; the incident has very much shaken him. He cares for her, you must know it.'

'In his way,' she sighed.

'To each his own, Dominique.'

He had never spoken her name before and the speaking of it made her very aware of the deep, slightly grating timbre of his voice. It was the kind of voice suited to him, holding the gritty deeps of his nature.

'You think they are suited, *signore*?'

'Two of the beautiful people, with volatile emotions. I expect it worried you that Tony went to pieces—your sister thought it was he who offered the comfort of his shoulder, eh?'

She nodded and felt his fingers holding her own shoulder, imparting into her bones a sensation that was on the edge of pain; not physical pain exactly, but as if a flame licked at her body. She couldn't define the feeling and put it down to the alarm which his height and his darkness seemed to generate whenever he was near her.

'You've been very considerate,' she said shakily. 'I—I do thank you, *signore*.'

'There is no need for thanks.' His fingers slid to her wrist. 'Come, let me escort you to your room, where you must promise me that you will get straight into your bed and go to sleep. You will do that?'

'I'll try——'

'I insist on it. I can feel that you're rocking on your feet.'

Her legs felt most unsteady, so she didn't resist when he slid an arm about her waist and took her weight as they walked in the direction of her bedroom. He had comforted Candice last night and it felt—nice to be comforted herself.

At the door of her room she pulled away from him. 'I shall be all right now——'

'Perhaps I should come inside and make sure you get into bed.' He gazed down at her, a wicked little glint showing in his eyes, there beneath a strand of his hair that was black as sin.

Her heart jolted and she hastily sought the door handle. 'You must do no such thing,' she opened the door and slid quickly inside her room. 'You must go and get some rest yourself—please do so.'

He lifted his cigar and took a deep pull. Then he gave that courteous, slightly Renaissance bow of his and in his long dark robe looked almost of those times, when men fought duels for the honour of their house and like Dante sometimes loved women with a fiercely celibate love.

'*Revedremo,*' he murmured, 'for now.'

She closed her door on his tall figure and then stood just inside her room with her hands pressed to her face. She envisioned him walking away, cigar smoke eddying back over his shoulder, perhaps a slight smile on his lips . . . the smile of a worldly man for an un-worldly woman.

His image persisted as Dominique removed her robe, kicked off her slippers and slid between the covers she had abandoned . . . oh, it seemed ages ago. She plumped her pillows and settled down with a weary yawn. Her eyelids grew heavy and she floated dreamily on the verge of sleep. It was rather like bath-ing in the surf at the edge of the sea, wafted between the shallows and the deeps.

She could feel herself drifting out into the deeps, carried there half willingly, yet with a part of her pull-ing back towards the unexciting shallows.

A sudden start shook her half awake . . . she had the feeling that her bedroom door had opened and that someone had looked in upon her. She felt the beat of her heart and imagined that Malina had stood there an instant in her doorway, a silent figure with a basilisk gaze, not a tinge of colour to warm the marble chill of her skin.

Dominique drew the bedcovers around her ... suddenly it seemed to her that Malina reminded her of a drowned woman she had seen in her student days, lying there in the hospital mortuary, white like marble, long hair dark with water, reddened rims to the eyes and nostrils. The sight had haunted her. She had been young and new to nursing ... and the finality of death.

Malina had saved Tony from such a death. He had grown up to be vital and handsome, and with an eye for girls like Candy.

Dominique pressed her face into her pillow ... she felt alone in her misgivings, and she felt afraid for Candice. She felt quite certain that Malina hated anyone who loved Antonio Romanos.

CHAPTER FIVE

BEYOND the smooth sands, pale and shining as bleached bones, the sea was a restless infinity of blue. It was a sheltered beach, tucked in under the cliffs that rose in weathered tiers to the Villa Dolorita which stood so serenely in the sunlight yet held within its tawny walls a confliction of loves and loyalties.

Almost two weeks had gone by since Candice had been so sick, and this morning as she lay at ease on a beach rug she had a tinge of colour in her cheeks and her eyes were almost as blue as the sky. Her dark moods had grown less frequent and she had shown a lot of improvement in her general condition. She now looked forward to these visits to the beach, but she hadn't yet plucked up the nerve to enter the sea.

'No, don't make me!' she would say, when Dominique urged her to float about in the shallows and get the feel of her legs.

'It's all right for you,' she would add. 'You don't know what it feels like, Nicky, to have no life in your legs. Just let me lie here and look at the water—you go in and have a swim.'

Dominique was a good swimmer, though she had refused to wear one of Candy's skimpy outfits and had gone into the local village to try and buy a bathing suit which she felt was more suitable. She had been lucky and found a shop which sold an assortment of rather outmoded goods including sunhats, paddling shoes and the kind of swimwear any girl but Dominique would have laughingly rejected. But Dominique was happy with her one-piece suit in a rather faded shade of ginger and she bought with it a sunhat adorned with some cockleshells, and a pair of sandals.

When she first changed into her beach outfit Candice couldn't stop giggling.

'You look,' she laughed, 'like one of Mack Sennett's Bathing Beauties!'

'My outfit isn't that ancient,' Dominique protested, unaware of her slim, long-legged grace as she ran down the beach into the water, striking out at once with the almost animal joy which a good swimmer experiences in the sea. The girls at St Anselma's had been taught to swim at the local baths and Dominique had taken to it because, unlike Candice, she hadn't minded getting her hair wet. Candice had always objected to damp straggly hair and water in her eyes . . . she was catlike in her love of comfort and good grooming.

So for several hours each day Candice sunbathed while Dominique took a swim and then read to her sister; her own skin was taking on a light tan and she felt remarkably well despite her constant concern and attention to Candy's wants.

'Italian weather has a kind of balm to it,' she remarked, putting aside *Pride and Prejudice* which they had just started, having enjoyed enormously their previous novel, a beautiful story by Sara Seale entitled *The Gentle Prisoner*. Candice had adored it, with almost a kind of wistfulness. 'Do people really find such loving happiness after stress?' she had asked. Dominique had been unable to give her a satisfactory answer but had said simply that lovely, imaginative writing was one of the pleasures of life and must be accepted on those terms, like the sea and the sands and the feel of a soft wind. Gentle things, when such elements were feeling gentle, and also stimulating.

Love? She didn't dare to define it but suspected that it could be as unpredictable as the sea and the wind; as stormy and as overwhelming if its mood should be so inclined.

'You like Italy, don't you?' Candice sifted the soft pale sand through her fingers, piling it into a little pyramid.

'It's a beautiful place,' Dominique agreed, gazing out at the sea where the long swooping tide was beginning to darken the edge of the beach. Soon it would be time for them to return to the villa. Don Presidio always knew when to come loping down the cliff steps in time to lift Candice and carry her home. Tony never came for her. His aversion to the sea was such that he couldn't bear to be within sight of it, but he was always there at the top of the cliffs to take Candy into his arms, in a kind of relay that gave his brother a chance to catch his breath.

It strangely impressed Dominique that the brothers

never relegated this task to any of the male servants. 'Here you are, brother,' the Don would say, and with the brief smile that creased the skin beside his eyes he would place Candice carefully in Tony's arms and the tide wind would catch at her pale golden hair and flick it against her husband's cheek.

This was one of the images which Dominique would eventually carry home with her. One day she would have to leave to pick up the threads of her own life; her sister was growing stronger and more confident and there was always the hope that she would recover her full strength.

'Here comes the tide,' she murmured. 'Soon your knights will come to carry you to the castle.'

'Nicky——' Candice looked directly at her sister, whose own flaxen hair had been darkened by her dip in the sea, making a sort of cap around the quiet oval of her face. Her spectacles were halfway down her nose so she looked owlish and wise. 'I sometimes think you're as romantic as I am—why don't you confess your terrible secret?'

Dominique smiled and the sea-light concealed the expression in her grey eyes. 'I expect I'm romantic in a different way.'

'Meaning?'

'Meaning, my dear Candy, that romance for you is centred in a man.'

'Isn't that where it should be centred?' Candice tilted her head to one side and kept her gaze fixed upon Dominique's face. 'That is the natural way of things, surely?'

'Are you telling me that I'm unnatural?' Dominique smiled slightly, for she already knew the answer to her question. Candice rejected with every atom of her body the chastity which Dominique intended for herself.

'It isn't *you* that's unnatural,' said Candice, with a snap in her voice. 'It's what you intend to do with yourself that doesn't make sense. Nicky, stay here in Italy! Stay at the villa for always—Presidio won't mind! Look at the way he's allowed Malina to make it her home——'

'I'm not Malina.' A shadow passed over Dominique's face. 'We both know that I can't stay indefinitely—one day soon you'll be back on your feet and then you must convince Tony that the two of you must start that dancing school you spoke about. I think it's a great idea——'

'If I get back on my feet.' A moody look crept into Candy's eyes, darkening the blue of her gaze. 'I think I'm always going to be this way and because of it I—I'll lose Tony in the end. His patience will run out and he'll go to that other woman for good!'

'Candy, there is no other woman——'

'There is, and I should know.' Tears crept into Candy's eyes. 'I tell you I know that he goes to visit someone. He goes when I'm supposed to be sleeping in the afternoons. I hear his Lancia drive away from the house and I lie there counting the minutes and the hours—you can't know what it does to me, Nicky! You've never loved a man! Love isn't in the heart, it's in the gut, and that's where it can twist and turn and tear you apart just like a living pain.'

'Don't upset yourself.' Dominique leaned forward and dabbed away the tears from her sister's face. 'Look, my dear, if what you think is true, then perhaps it might be best if you came home to England with me? You could, you know.'

'I—I can't leave him.' Candice drew her lower lip between her teeth. 'I've thought about it, but when I see him, when he's so nice to me at times, I melt inside and I want to be with him—even if it kills me!'

'Oh, Candy, I——'

'That's the way love can make you feel,' Candice said fiercely. 'As if once you're in it and you care all the way through, then you just have to belong to the man who's hurting you. Th-that's the silly way women are made! You love a man a-and hate him at the same time because you know he's up to something. You try to break away and at the same time you keep hoping that everything will come right and be heavenly, but instead it goes on being a kind of heaven and hell all mixed up. If I left Tony I'd be even more miserable. I have to be near him—I have to see him and touch him. You just don't understand that part of it, Nicky.'

Dominique gazed at the sea and its relentless approach . . . somehow it gave her an image of what love for a man could be like if a woman allowed it to have its sway over her. With a kind of fateful force it could suddenly be too close to be escaped; before you could turn and run it could be upon you, overwhelming you in its dark, shining lustre.

She jumped to her feet as if the tide was suddenly touching her toes; it wasn't, for it had only just reached the rocks at the edge of the beach and was lapping at them.

'Don Presidio seems a little late today.' She heard the rather off-key note in her voice. 'I hope he hasn't forgotten us!'

Candice cast a startled look at the cliff steps, winding like a snake up the towering side of them. She glanced at the gold bangled watch on her wrist, then at the sea where the spume was growing a little more turbulent.

'What shall we do?' she gasped. 'If he doesn't come——?'

Dominique shaded her eyes from the sun and gazed

up the cliffside. In less than ten minutes the tide would be up the beach and her sister was unable to walk.

'I—I'd have to drag you to the steps and try and get you up beyond the danger point,' she said. 'We were talking about novels, weren't we? They say truth is more dramatic than fiction! I can't leave you to go and fetch a man to carry you, and I can't carry you myself. I could support you in the water, but I—I don't know for how long.'

'Nicky,' it was a whisper and yet it was a cry, 'do you think he's forgotten on purpose?'

'Candy!'

'Why not?' Candice said wildly. 'I'm nothing but a drag on Tony a-and there's always been some sort of talk about the way Amatrice lost her life. It was supposed to be an illness, but I've heard whispers that it was something else——'

'Don't say such a thing—don't even think it!' Dominique fell on to her knees and gripped Candice by the shoulders, giving her a shake. 'Don't get hysterical—any moment now he'll come running down those steps——'

'No, he won't.' Candice shook her head and there was panic in her eyes. 'Don't you see how easy it would be for him to leave us here? It would look like an accident—one sister too paralysed to walk, and the other too devoted to leave her. There wouldn't be a soul to say it was anything but a tragedy——'

'Stop it!' Dominique gave her a fiercer shake. 'We aren't going to perish on this damn beach, not if I can prevent it.'

'You swore, Nicky.'

'There are times when I do. Look, Candy, look at that sea—are you going to just lie there and let it sweep over you, or are you going to help me and yourself by getting to your feet?'

'How can I?' Candice wailed. 'I'm stuck here a-and we both know it!'

'I know nothing of the sort.' Suddenly a flame of determination was burning inside Dominique . . . this was what was called a moment of truth and Candice had to be made to take the bull by the horns. 'You don't want to drown, do you? You've always loved life, and if it's true that Tony's seeing another woman then why should you let that woman have him by lying here and letting the sea take you? All you have to do is get to your feet—come on, Candy, try! Take your first steps back to a new life and stop clinging to the old one that's taken all the sparkle out of you and left you subdued.'

'I—I can't do it,' Candice resisted the grip of Dominique's hands. 'He'll come—Presidio will come, he always does!'

'Take another look at the cliff steps and you'll see they're empty. Take another look at the tide and you'll see that it's beyond the rocks and rising fast. My dear, you've got to trust in me and stand up—come on, make the effort!'

'M-my legs just won't move—they won't move, Nicky!'

'Listen to me—that night you were taken sick I saw your legs move. I saw them and so did Don Presidio. Stop letting your mind decide for you; let your body do the work and it will! It truly will!'

'No.' Candice shook her head despairingly. 'Y-you go, Nicky, and leave me here—I don't care. What's there to live for?'

'A lot of things, all the things you loved to do, especially your dancing.' Dominique spoke urgently, for behind her she could hear the silken swish of the water as it advanced up the beach towards them. 'I can't leave you, so you're going to have to come with me. Now move, show some of the spunk you used to have—up with you!'

Candice cried out as Dominique gave a lunge that forced her into a sagging, almost upright heap, but so quivering and weak that she almost sent the pair of them toppling over. Dominique hung on grimly as they swayed and almost fell. 'That's it, darling,' she panted, and with her jaw set she took on the task of getting her sister to the cliffside steps before the tide swept them off their feet.

If that should happen she knew there was a limit to how long her strength could support Candice in the water. In the old days Candice had been the more curvaceous of the two of them, but sickness had wasted some of the flesh from her bones; all the same Dominique was still the slighter of the two and it took all her tenacity to half drag, half support her sister on that seemingly long haul to the steps, and once there she had to strain and beg Candice to try and lift her feet off the sand.

'Y-you can do it,' she panted. 'W-we've got this far, so try and help me to get you a little farther.'

'I——' Candice struggled, tears ebbing down her cheeks as she blundered and clutched at the steps, 'I wish you'd leave me—oh, leave me alone a-and don't make me——'

'I've got to make you,' Dominique said fiercely . . . oh God, why hadn't the Don come down to the beach today? What could have delayed him? He knew that when the tide turned it took only a short time for the sea to cover the sands and then rise several feet up the cliffside. Holy Mary, how was she going to get Candice that far out of reach of the greedy water? They'd both drown, clinging together like a pair of sea waifs!

'Please, for your own sake,' she begged Candice, who struggled bravely, hitting her knees against the harsh stone and painfully scraping off the skin.

It had to be a miracle, but suddenly they had made it up one step, then two, and Dominique just wasn't sure any more if she was lifting and pulling Candice, or whether her sister was actually doing some of the work herself.

'Enough!' Suddenly from around a bend in the stone stairway the tall figure of the Don loomed into view; his eyes seemed to burn darkly in his rather pale face as he loped down to where they were and quickly gathered Candice up into his arms.

Dominique felt her heart turn over with relief . . . relief followed by a hot stab of anger.

'Where have you been?' she cried out. 'We thought you weren't coming and poor Candice——'

Candice was sobbing against his shoulder and clinging to him as if he were a solid spar she had suddenly come to grips with in the churning sea which was now flooding the beach.

'I wouldn't have let either of you drown.' His teeth seemed to bite on the words, strong and white against his skin which still held that curious look of pallor. 'I had to find out if your sister would have the guts to get this far—well, it looks as if both Davis sisters have guts and tenacity, doesn't it?'

'You mean——?' Dominique gazed up at him in total disbelief. 'You've been lurking up here all the time— watching us *struggle*?'

He inclined his head. 'I had the idea that if you were left alone together with the tide coming in fast, you would find a way to get to the steps. I was right, was I not?'

Grey eyes blazed at him, for in that violent effort to reach the steps Dominique had lost her spectacles and that, she realised, was why she hadn't spotted the Don. To aid his concealment he was wearing a dark shirt and trousers, and she told herself wildly that he looked the devil that he was.

'I—I think I hate you!' she gasped. 'Have you any idea——?'

'I think so, *signorina*.'

'I think *not*, *signore*. I'd be obliged if you'll carry my sister up to the house while I look for my glasses——'

'My good girl, you can't do that!' His voice rang out. 'They are now under water.'

'As we might have been.' She glanced over her shoulder and saw hazily that the water had swept over the beach rug where Candice had lain and by now had carried off *Pride and Prejudice*, their tin of biscuits and her spectacles. She vaguely remembered them falling off her nose as she had hoisted Candice to her feet . . . now she was feeling the aches and bruises of that maddened scramble to beat the tide, with fear beating at her mind as the water beat at the rocks.

'I think I quite hate you, Don Presidio,' she said clearly. 'I think you're probably the most ruthless man I've ever met in my life!'

'You're probably right,' he agreed, 'but this is not the time nor the place to discuss my perfidious nature. We'll leave that for another occasion, eh?'

Dominique glared at his back and his long legs as she followed him with his burden to the top of the cliffs . . . right now she was in no mood to judge him as anything but a monster for allowing Candice and herself to suffer those awful, endless minutes when it had seemed as if he had deserted them.

She felt as if she had been put through a wringer,

emotionally and physically, and when they reached the clifftop she felt as if her tired legs would buckle.

'Where's Tony?' She glanced about her, but he was nowhere to be seen. 'Oh no, is he playing tricks with us as well?'

'Tony was sent off on an errand by me,' the Don threw over his shoulder. Candice lay very quietly in his arms, with her head resting against him, and with an alarmed leap of her pulse Dominique checked to see that her sister hadn't fainted.

Candice partly opened her blue eyes and a faint smile touched her lips. 'I did move my legs, didn't I?' she said. 'I *felt* them move.'

'Are you feeling all right, dear?' Dominique asked anxiously.

Candice nodded. 'I'm sleepy.'

'I should think so, after that marathon!' Dominique smiled her relief, for there was in that smile of Candy's a hint of the mischief that used to be there.

'Don't fuss,' the Don chided, as he strode with Candice along the path that led through the enormous garden to the house. 'This girl is better than she has been for a long time—her mind has woken up her body, and that was what she needed.'

'I just don't like tricks, Don Presidio.' Dominique spoke severely, but all the same his ruthless method had seemed to work ... if Candice could be persuaded to try her legs again and not be disheartened that they would be weak and unwilling for a while and would need massage and a lot of exercise.

'There are times when it's necessary to dice in the face of the gods,' he rejoined, 'and to hope that they won't strike us dead for our audacity. I meant well; believe that if you can't believe anything else.'

As he spoke he increased his stride and Dominique

felt too exhausted to try and keep up with him. The breath trembled through her lips and she felt so limp that she just had to pause and rest for a moment on one of the garden seats. She drew a hand across her forehead and found it damp with sweat . . . she was the one who suddenly felt faint, and leaning forward with her head between her knees she breathed deeply and felt the garden swim around her.

It was a most unpleasant feeling and she was glad when it ebbed away; she continued to rest for a few more minutes. Candice would be all right for a while; her maid would be summoned and she'd be cosseted and given a nice cup of tea.

As much as Dominique yearned for a cup of tea herself, she couldn't yet make the effort to go indoors. Her gaze rested upon a nearby clump of wicked looking zinnias and she heard the buzzing of honeybees and the big green-backed flies. Pale-purple bells of campanula dangled over a wall and the bitter-sweetness of fig trees mingled with the tang of pomegranates and lemons.

She gave quite a start when all at once the Don's manservant hovered over her, neat in his grey jacket, and presented her with just the medicine she needed right now.

'The *signore* said you would be needing this, *signorina*.' A cup of tea stood upon a round silver tray.

'Oh—*grazie*.' Dominique accepted it with a trembling hand. She caught a whiff of cognac in the tea, and felt puzzled by the complexity of the man who could put her through a form of torture and then give her tea to soothe her racked nerves. A part of her felt like sending back the message that he go to hell, but already her lips were at the rim of the cup and never had tea tasted so heavenly.

'The *signorina* is quite all right?' The manservant was giving her a rather concerned look, one which informed her that never before had he seen the neat and capable Nurse Davis looking as if she had been pulled backward through several hedges.

'I'm fine, thank you.' She managed a smile. 'I'll just drink my tea, then come indoors.'

'*Si*.' He made his way back to the house, where no doubt he would inform the other members of the staff that the English nurse was looking a little odder than usual this morning.

And what a morning, the tidal breeze softly blowing her hair and the air smelling of wild, lost places—Atlantis—Shangri La—the Garden of Eden.

Fancies, she thought wryly, as she sipped her tea. Prosaic tea for the English nurse as she sat in an Italian garden and let her imagination have its way with her. There had been in her busy life too little time for dreaming . . . and never had she imagined that she'd live through a kind of nightmare which a man had deliberately arranged.

Yet . . . she half-smiled, to give the devil his due the ploy had worked. Candice had revealed the will to walk, to live and be again the girl she had been.

Then, Dominique thought, I shall return to England and all this will have become the setting of a dream I once had. The people who played a part in that dream will fade like old photographs and I shall never see Don Presidio again.

She sat there, grey eyes staring as if into a void.

The realisation was a hurting thing and she had no right to feel this way. It was an indication that the sooner Candice was back on her feet the better for both of them. The threads of both their lives could be picked up again, and hers lay woven in a design from which men were excluded. Especially a man such as the Don!

Then, as if her thoughts had conjured him, he was halfway along the path to where she sat, his long strides bringing him there before she could rise and run for cover among the trees. Her heart raced and she felt as scared as a hare that sees the fox and can't run ... how dark he was in the morning sunlight, his dark clothing adding to his Machiavellian looks. A moment more and he was standing above her, darkly sculptured by the golden sunlight, and his gaze was so penetrating it seemed to pierce her skin.

'Have you had time to reflect?' he asked, his voice deep and sonorous. 'Now do you realise that sometimes to be kind one has to be cruel?'

'Is—is Candice all right?' Dominique strove with all her will to meet calmly the dark lustre of his eyes. 'She's with her maid?'

'Stop worrying about her,' he ordered. 'Has there ever been a time, Nurse, when you have paused for five minutes to worry about yourself? Or don't you think you are worth wasting time over?'

'You know the saying,' she said evasively, 'the devil finds work for idle hands, and I'm sure he puts foolishness into idle minds.'

'What foolishness, I wonder, has he put into your mind while you've been sitting here drinking that beverage the English regard as a kind of cure-all?'

'Oh—you can guess what I've been thinking.'

'Can I?' His eyes searched hers. 'How well can you see without your spectacles?'

'Only hazily—luckily the ones I lost were my tinted pair for wearing in the sunshine. My others are in my room.'

'I must pay for you to have a new pair of tinted spectacles, as it was my fault you lost them.'

'It doesn't matter.'

'That wasn't your sentiment when you told me you hated me and thought me the most ruthless person you had ever met. Strong sentiments for a girl who plans to take the veil.'

'Well, I'm no saint, *signore*.'

'I'm relieved to hear it.' A smile flickered on his lips. 'I have no liking for sanctimonious women.'

As he said the words and stood above her she saw in his stance the arrogance that was part of him, his heritage from forebears who had sought privilege and power from a royalist system which had encouraged men to seek their fortunes boldly, providing they shared it with the princes. Long dead was such a system, but Dominique knew that the man who faced her carried those old instincts in his veins and at times the daring and the ruthlessness came to the surface.

Right now she sensed those instincts pulsing in him, warm and strong as the blood pulsing through his powerful body. A kind of fear was welded to her fascination as she watched him and saw how the dark shirt had thrust itself open against the brown column of his neck. Unlike Tony he didn't wear a religious medal on a chain. Lack of vanity, she told herself, rather than a basic lack of belief in the power of good over devilment. A devil he could be, but in a good cause it would seem. A complex man, with as many wild and secretive places in his nature as in the garden of his house.

'Are you trying to see into me?' he asked, almost casually.

'Th-that would be asking a lot.' She felt a fluttering in her throat and put her hand to it.

'Not too much I think. What do you see, Nurse, when you look at me with your hazy grey eyes?'

'I see a man——'

'This gets interesting,' his lips mocked, 'so do go on.'

'A man, Don Presidio, of strength and a ruthless kind of determination. I see the past in you, when the Medici dukes were in power. Unlike your brother Tony you are something of a throwback.'

'There is one in every family,' he drawled. 'In the Davis family it's yourself. Your sister is very much of these modern times, but you are not. Let me place you,' he considered her, hoisting a foot upon the edge of the garden seat and considering her by leaning down a little, a position which she found even more alarming.

'How about the Nurse in *Romeo and Juliet*?' she murmured. 'Wouldn't that be appropriate?'

'How about Juliet herself?'

'That would be beyond the realms of possibility, *signore*. Juliet was beautiful.'

'Juliet, *signorina*, was wide-eyed and romantic, and she fell in love from a balcony. Wouldn't that describe you?'

'I'm not on a balcony, and how can a nurse be romantic when she sees only the realistic side of life?'

'All the same, Nurse, the fact that you believe in faith, hope and heaven makes you a romantic. How many people these days believe in that trilogy?'

'You ask me that, *signore*, because you happen to be a cynic?'

'Are you so sure of that, *signorina*? I surely hoped that your sister would put up a fight to walk if she found herself in danger.' His eyes narrowed. 'Or is it possible that you thought I had left the pair of you to drown?'

'The thought did cross my mind,' she admitted.

'And why so, may I ask?'

'Because you seemed to regard Candice as a burden

upon your brother.'

'And you thought I'd go to the extreme of letting the pair of you drown? I'm well aware, of course, that you would have stayed by her side had you not been able to get her to those steps.'

'They were fraught moments.' A shiver ran over Dominique's sensitive skin. 'It was rather like a nightmare and I——I didn't dream that you were putting us through it on purpose.'

'So ruthless of me, eh?'

'Yes.'

'Men can be that way.'

'It would seem so.'

'Am I not to be forgiven? All of us, after all "being by nature born in sin, and the children of wrath." '

She gave him a surprised look and saw a smile twitch his lips.

'Don't forget my Jesuit college; I was sent there early and taught that the sins of the flesh lead to hellfire and damnation. In short, that the devil is a woman.'

'But you——' she blinked, for his gaze was as disturbing as a ray of hot sunlight. 'You don't strike me as a man of dark superstitions, and yet——'

'And yet, *signorina*?'

'Perhaps there is something pagan in you.'

'It's in all of us at certain times. In you as well, little nun.'

'D-don't call me that!' she begged.

'Why not, pray? Isn't it relevant?'

'Not in that tone of voice.'

'I had no idea that my tone of voice was——offensive.'

'Not offensive b-but jibing.' A flush of colour came into her cheeks. 'You know what I mean, so don't pretend——'

'Perhaps you are the one who's pretending.' His

eyelids drooped as he watched her, and yet she sensed a kind of alertness in him ... as of a tiger stalking through a forest, scenting its prey and ready to pounce at the most unexpected moment. It put Dominique on the alert and she could feel the tension in herself. 'Why should I pretend?' she asked.

'Perhaps because of a misapprehension,' he replied.

'Oh, what about?' Tensed as a coiled spring she sat there, ready at any moment to bound to her feet.

'That because you never happened to appeal to the callow young men who courted your pink and white sister you came to the conclusion that you were unappealing to all men. Young men often see only the icing and not the cake, and because your sister had the candy coating that attracts the sweet tooth, it never occurred to you that there are men whose teeth wish to bite into something a little more satisfying than candy can be.'

When making an explicit statement his strong, white teeth seemed to bite upon the words, so that for Dominique her tiger analogy was even more vivid and threatening. She put a hand to her throat as if feeling those strong teeth in her neck.

'Come, would you really have wanted a retinue of callow young men?' he drawled.

'No,' she said honestly. 'But you see—no one ever kissed me.'

Dominique would never know what made her say such a thing to him ... to Don Presidio Romanos of all people!

'Ah,' he said very softly, and just as she thought the moment of danger had passed he seized hold of her and swung her bodily off the garden seat. 'That can soon be remedied.' He pulled her forcibly against him. 'Let me kiss you!'

Dominique felt his hard, dark closeness; she heard what he said, but she hung suspended between the reality of being seized and the unreality of believing it had happened. 'W-what are you doing——?'

'This!' He tilted her over his arm into a posture of helplessness and then she felt the sudden heat of his mouth on hers. The heat and the pressure were real and her heart thumped. When she tried to struggle her feet came off the ground and she was entirely in his arms.

'Be still!' His lips travelled round to the side of her neck and then downwards into the opening of her shirt . . . her cry of protest was again muffled by his mouth and the more she writhed and pummelled him, the more persistent he was in his kissing. It seemed as if he would kiss the breath right out of her body . . . as if he meant to make her faint.

When he stood her on her feet she swayed and clutched at him, dizzy with confusion. He stood very close, looking down at her, the black hair streaking his forehead. He didn't speak, and Dominique was incapable of speech for the moment. When she realised that she was gripping his arm, she hastily let go and backed away from him. She had no idea how huge were the pupils of her eyes, nor for the moment was she aware that her struggles had wrenched open most of her shirt.

'I—I don't need that kind of therapy——' The words caught breathlessly in her throat.

'Therapy?' he mocked. 'What a very clinical word for something that is supposed to be pleasurable!'

'I didn't find it very pleasurable——'

'Indeed? Then what sensations did it arouse?'

'Disagreeable ones.'

'H'm, then I must be losing my touch.'

'Have you touched lots of women?' She gave a scornful toss of the head; her strength was coming back and her sense of outraged dignity.

'Most of the females in San Sabina,' he drawled.

'Th-there's no need to be sarcastic!'

'Why ever not, when you've had the temerity to call my lovemaking disagreeeable?'

'You forced me—I didn't want your kissing!' Wild colour shaded her cheekbones and her lips looked stung; her skin in the gaping neck of her shirt showed some of that blush.

'When a girl tells a man that she's never been kissed, then she's asking for the obvious.'

'I wasn't—I didn't mean—as if I would!'

'You mean you weren't inviting me to kiss you?' He raised a mocking eyebrow. 'How crushing for my ego!'

'You knew I wasn't inviting you—it just slipped out.' Her cheeks felt hot and she had realised her dishevelment and with unsteady fingers was trying to do up the buttons he had somehow forced open with his mouth.

'Shall I do that?' he enquired. 'I'm not quite so shaken up as you appear to be.'

'Let me be!' She thrust his hand away and her eyes shot sparks at him. 'W-what I said just slipped out and that's all there was to it.'

'Most Freudian remarks just slip out—those buttons are done up lopsidedly.'

'They'll do, a-and I wasn't making a Freudian remark as you call it.'

'Permit me to contradict you, Nurse.' He seemed to purr the words deep in the depths of that brown-skinned throat which he made no attempt to cover up. 'We all like to believe that we're in control of our every thought and action, but it isn't really the case. There's a part of us that lurks in secret places in our psyche and at unexpected moments it leaps out to take us by surprise. It's called the subconscious and you as a nurse can't deny its existence. Look what it did to Candice.'

Dominique passed the tip of her tongue over her lips, which had a swollen feel to them. She felt and was sure she looked as if she'd been *used*, whereas he . . . her gaze flickered over his powerful frame in the dark silk shirt, and the trousers that fitted close to his lean hips and legs without giving him that look of display she had noticed in his brother, as if Tony were about to step on to a dance floor and go into Latin-American tango routine.

'I do so want Candice to get fit again,' Dominique said fervently. 'She owes it to herself and to Tony.'

'And to you, of course.'

Dominique lifted her gaze to his face. 'Yes,' she agreed.

'You have your life to live, don't you?'

He said it so sardonically that she bit her lip. 'As we all have, *signore*.'

'If it can be called living for a young woman to cover her hair with a veil and lock up all her natural desires. All very good for the soul, but you have a body as well. Can you ignore your body, or do you intend to scourge it?'

'I intend not to discuss my—not with you.'

'How disappointing!' He stood there with his hands in his pockets and the sun warming his skin, blending with its Latin darkness. 'So if your sister now proves to be on the mend, you will soon be leaving my ménage?'

'Yes, I'm only here for her sake.' Dominique glanced shortsightedly at her watch. 'It's time I went to her.'

'I so dislike the look of that cheap watch on your

wrist,' he said. 'I think you should allow me to replace
it with a good one. It may be the last present a man
will give you.'

'The first and last,' she corrected him.

'There you go again, Nurse!' His lip quirked.
'You're in danger of having an inferiority complex.'

'You aren't, are you?' She fiercely told herself that
she didn't want *anything* from him . . . she didn't want
reminders of the way he looked and spoke and could
twist the nerves deep in her body. 'I'd be afraid of
damaging a good watch, *signore*. I prefer this one.'

His dark brows drew together. 'Don't be so damned
independent!'

'Don't touch me——!' She backed sharply away, for
though he didn't make a move she had sensed the intention. 'I won't let you—not again!'

'Who are you frightened of?' He gave a brief laugh.
'Yourself or me?'

'I don't like being used for your amusement—you
make me feel cheap!'

'To match the watch which you prefer, eh?'

'You twist everything I say!'

'On the contrary, Nurse, I try to straighten you out,
but you keep flying out of reach and blundering with
those shortsighted eyes into a web made of nun's
veiling. You make me fume—I'd like to shake some
sense into you!'

The threat of it was in every line of him, and
Dominique didn't wait to find out if he would grab
hold of her and apply one of those strong hands to her
shoulder. She turned and ran, blundering along the
path that led to the house. She couldn't see clearly and
when she reached the steps leading up to the courtyard
she miscalculated and tripped, tried to steady herself
and fell sprawling on her hands and knees.

'Ouch!' Even as contact with the stony ground stung her knees, a pair of hands jerked her to her feet ... hands which had touched her before and transmitted the same feeling as now, an electrifying tingle that seemed to run all the way down her body to the ends of her toes, curling them.

CHAPTER SIX

'I'M all right!' She struck at his hand and tried to squirm out of his grasp. 'Don't do that!'

He was dusting her down and quizzing one of her knees which had started to bleed.

'Come along, I'll take you indoors while you are still in one piece.' Gripping her by the elbow, the Don proceeded to walk her across the courtyard and into the hall. 'Attend to that scraped knee before you start nursing someone else,' he ordered. 'Can you manage the stairs without falling down them, you little bat?'

'I-I'd have my glasses if it wasn't for you.' She dragged free of him and gave him a stormy look from beneath a tousled wing of hair. 'I hope Candice doesn't have some kind of reaction from being so scared by what you put her through.'

'Did I scare you?' he asked, looking amused rather than contrite.

'Of course I was scared. I didn't know what you were up to.'

'No, you assumed that I was going to see the pair of you drown like unwanted kittens. Your opinion of me isn't very charitable, is it? Well, I don't think your sister has come to much harm—quite the reverse. Take

a little more care of yourself, Nurse, and don't forget
to put some iodine on that knee.'

His eyes raked her up and down, then he turned on
his heel and strode off in the direction of his study.
Dominique made her way upstairs, holding wearily to
the banister rail. Her knees hurt and her muscles ached
and she felt all churned up inside. Life in the vicinity
of Don Presidio was about as tranquil as living in a
cage with a tiger. His vigour and challenge seemed to
stir the air and bring to the surface the feelings she
had submerged since those days when she'd watch
Candice go off to dance while she settled down to
cheese on toast and the nurses' manual.

Dominique entered her room and was glad to shut
the world outside for a short while. She sank down on
the bed, removed her sandals and reached for a
Kleenex so she could wipe the blood from her knee.

The events of the morning persisted in her thoughts
. . . she couldn't seem to forget the struggle to get
Candy on her feet, nor finding herself in a man's arms
and so weak in contrast to his strength. Her mind held
a vivid image of those moments when she had hung
there in the sinewy brown arms, her heart hammering
and any cry she might have given choked off by the
crush of his lips on hers. She still seemed to feel the
aquiline thrust of his nose against her face, the determined way he held her to his hard body, the reckless
force with which he had kissed her.

She ran a finger back and forth across her bottom
lip, she felt the sensitivity there and a resurgence of
the disturbances which contact with his firm flesh and
hard bones had brought to life in the quiet cloisters of
her body.

'No!' She jumped to her feet, grabbed her sponge bag
and her uniform and made for the bathroom that was

just along the corridor from her room. Once inside and under the shower she scrubbed her body from head to toe . . . a scourging which couldn't reach into her mind. There the memories were still very much alive, and even when she had put on her uniform, combed her hair into its usual neatness and replaced her spectacles on her nose, she could still see her own helpless captivity in the Don's arms . . . could feel beneath her scrubbed skin the secret nerves still tingling.

'Drat the man!' She flung her sponge at the mirror and spattered her neat image with water . . . she didn't feel her usual neat and composed self inside and it took something of an effort to look cool, calm and collected when she entered her sister's bedroom.

Candice was comfortably arranged on the lounger between the windows, smiling a little to herself in a bedjacket trimmed with white fur.

'I'm going to walk again, aren't I, Nicky?'

'Yes,' Dominique said firmly. 'You should be looking pleased with yourself.'

'You did it, Nicky—oh, I'll never forget how I felt when my poor legs actually moved. They did, didn't they? I wasn't dreaming it?'

'You weren't dreaming, pet, but I can't take all the credit. It was Don Presidio's idea to leave us on the beach with the tide coming in . . . his brand of shock treatment.'

Candice gazed wide-eyed at Dominique. 'You mean—he did that to us on purpose?'

Dominique inclined her head. 'He didn't just appear on the scene to scoop you up in his manly arms, my dear. He was in hiding, waiting to see if I could get you to move. It worked, of course, but what a Machiavellian way to go about it. I—I suppose had he confided his intention to me, I might have been less maddened in my efforts to get you on your feet—he's quite ruthless, of course.'

Candice sat there and cradled her arms about herself. 'He puts your back up, doesn't he, Nicky?'

'He does!' she said fervently. 'I won't be sorry to see the back of him!'

'Honestly?' Candice had her blue eyes fixed upon Dominique's face. 'Don't you feel anything for men? I mean—don't you want a man to touch you, or hold you?'

'It would hardly do for me to want—those sort of things.' Dominique went briskly to the bedside and fetched the thermometer from the tumbler where it stood. She gave it a shake and approached Candice with it. 'Open up.'

'Perhaps you ought to have your temperature taken, Nicky.'

'Why?'

'There's a flush in your cheeks. You look—sort of different, do you know that?'

'It's just that I'm pleased about you.' Dominique inserted the thermometer between her sister's lips before she could say anything more that could add to the unsettled state of her nerves. 'I'm going to insist that you take things easy for the rest of the day, but tomorrow—tomorrow, Candy, you're going to try those legs again.'

Candy's pulse quickened under Dominique's fingers and she looked both eager and apprehensive. 'Suppose I can't—walk?' she said, watching as the thermometer was checked.

'You'd better make a good effort,' Dominique advised, 'or you'll have your brother-in-law thinking up another of his alarming ploys. He should have lived in the days of the Borgias when the factions were always plotting and conniving. Anyway, despite the morning's trauma you're in quite good condition. Your heart isn't racing and you haven't a fever. Pleased with yourself, little sister?'

Candice nodded and reclined her fair head against the satin pillows of the lounger. She looked extremely pretty, reminding Dominique of what the Don had said about Candy being the pink and white sister, the one with the icing who attracted young men with a sweet tooth.

'If you love Tony,' she said quietly, 'the time has come for you to fight for him back.'

Dominique went to the dressing-table and picked up the silver-backed hand mirror and brought it to Candice. She held it so her sister could see herself.

'Do you know who you look like right now?' she asked.

A smile quivered on Candy's lips as she shook her head.

'Do you remember those movie magazines I used to collect when we shared our flat? Those lovely plump ones from the old days of Hollywood, which I still have stored away in a cupboard? One of them had a stunning picture of Jean Harlow on the cover, and that's who you resemble, Candy. I don't see how Tony can possibly want any other woman when he has you— you hang on to that thought and it will do you more good than any medicine or therapy.'

Candice took the hand mirror and studied her face and hair intently. 'Jean Harlow was a sex goddess, wasn't she—and she died when she was twenty-six?'

'I only said you looked like her, so don't go brooding about any other kind of similarity. Now what do you fancy for your lunch? How about melon, a cheese omelette with salad, a glass of *vino santo* and a peach?'

Candice laughed, 'You sound like a waitress!'

'It might have been a less worrying occupation for me.'

'Never! You're a born nurse, Nicky. Oh, Nicky, don't go back to England when I get well! Don't go back to become—I'll never get to see you if you do that—that awful thing!'

'You mustn't call it that,' Dominique reproved. 'I know what I want——'

'Do you?' Candice stared at her. 'I've heard it said that women who take the veil are hiding from themselves.'

'That's nonsense!'

'I don't think it's so wide off the mark where some people are concerned,' Candice argued. 'But you've never been a sanctimonious, frigid sort of person, wrapped up in the idea that heaven isn't here on earth to be enjoyed, only the hard work that leads to it— when you're too worn out to care! D'you remember Sister St Clare? The poor old dear couldn't use her hands in the end, they were so crippled after years of having them steeped in the sink or the scrubbing bucket! Nicky, don't turn into another Sister St Clare!'

'You only remember her hands,' Dominique smiled. 'When I think of her I recall the tranquillity of her eyes. She was a happy woman, Candy, but you were too much of a child to realise it.'

'Well, it isn't my idea of happiness——' Candice broke off with a sigh. 'What is happiness, anyway? It isn't all that easy to find, is it? When I met Tony I thought I'd found it, but instead I've found out that I'm sharing him with someone else. I have to lie here and put up with it, but later on, when I'm really well, I won't be able to! I'll walk out on him sooner than lead that sort of life! Would you, Nicky?'

Dominique shook her head. 'I doubt it. I don't pretend to know anything about being in love, but I imagine it should be a devotion shared wholeheartedly by two people. But are you certain——?'

'I've asked Malina,' Candice confessed. 'I—I had to find out for sure and she knows him inside out—she doesn't like me, so she told me the truth. Tony visits someone on other the side of San Sabina.'

'You trust Malina to tell you the truth?' Dominique frowned.

'She enjoyed telling me—gloated over it. She leaned over my bed and told me there was a side to Tony I had never known about and would never understand because I'm the wrong sort of wife for him. She said he needed strength and had married weakness—it's true, Nicky, isn't it? She said it wasn't Tony who held me in his arms all that night I was so sick with fish poisoning, she said it was Presidio, but I wasn't to get any ideas about the *padrone* because she'd known him take care of a calf all night long.'

Silence ebbed and flowed in the room when Candice stopped speaking. It was as if a tide of realisation swept over both of them, tossing the truth at them like a stinging spray.

'The most important thing is that you walk again,' Dominique said at last. 'We'll try and sort things out when you're back on your feet, but right now I'll go and get your lunch. Do you fancy a *filet mignon*, or maybe a *pizza*?'

'A cheese omelette will do.' A little blue flame flickered in Candy's eyes. 'Don't forget my glass of wine.'

'I won't.' The sisters gazed steadily at each other for about half a minute and an observer would have seen in that moment a resemblance to each other; a touch of obstinacy in the set of the jaw.

As Dominique made her way downstairs she could feel a slackening of the nervous knots in her stomach. Candice had started to fight back, but whether or not her marriage would survive was problematical. She hated the image she had of Malina confiding to Candice that Tony was seeing someone else, but thank goodness it had stirred her sister up rather than cast her down.

No man, Dominique told herself, was worth a broken life. Life had to go on and it had to have some purpose to it ... love only had a purpose if it was a totally sharing thing.

Then, as she crossed the hall, she ran into Tony. He was carrying some flowers, a gorgeous spray of yellow roses. As Dominique's eyes lit on them she felt an impulse to knock them out of his hand. Now she knew how Candy had felt when she had struck him with the string of pearls.

'I saw these in the village and couldn't resist them.' He smiled disarmingly, showing his splendid teeth and looking darkly attractive in a slub silk shirt and well-tailored slacks. 'Presidio sent me on a mission of conciliation between two of the local wine-growers—what's the matter, Nicky? Is there anything wrong with Candice?'

'Would it very much matter to you?' she asked coldly.

'What do you mean?' A flash of pain showed in his fine dark eyes. 'You know I care what happens to Candy—she isn't ill again?'

'Physically she's fine, better than she has been for weeks. It's in her heart where she's hurting, Tony, and you know the reason for it. You've caused the heartburn.'

His gaze fell to the roses and he fingered one of the perfectly formed flowers. 'Nicky, I'd like to talk to you about that. Can you spare me some time today, perhaps after you've had your lunch?'

She didn't quite know what to say; what did he want to talk about that couldn't be discussed with his wife . . . surely not the possibility of a divorce? It had now become possible in Italy, but this was the household of a man who seemed to abide by the Catholic rules and once a week the local priest dined at his table. She had met Father Flavio herself and found him to be a charming man. She had the feeling that Presidio Romanos would demand of his brother that he abide by the marriage he had, she now realised, been warned not to attempt in the first place. Candice wasn't a Catholic, but Dominique herself had converted to that faith about five years ago.

'Does my sister come into what you want to talk about, Tony?' she asked, a note of reserve in her voice.

'Yes,' he inclined his head and there was a certain gravity in his eyes. 'May we meet in the gazebo at about two-thirty? Candy will be taking her rest at that time.'

'Is it about something that could hurt Candice?' Dominique couldn't keep a stilted note out of her voice; she felt she wanted to dislike him for the way he was hurting Candy, yet there was something a little sad in his eyes, almost a haunted look which tore her sympathies in two. Candice had trapped him into marrying her, but if at the time he had someone back here in Italy whom he cared for, then it had been wrong of him to take her sister to Paris on a romantic weekend. Candice had liked a good time but she hadn't been a good-time girl; she had gone with Tony because she had been head over heels in love with him.

'I'm afraid it is,' Tony admitted. 'Will you let me talk to you about it?'

'I don't quite know what to say——' She looked hesitant. 'I care very much for my sister; you know that, don't you?'

'*Si*, no one could be more caring than you, Nicky. You're a very understanding person, and that is why I need to talk with you. Please say you will listen!'

He looked so pleading, so somehow boyish in contrast to his self-confident brother whom, she doubted, would ask advice of an unmarried English girl.

'All right,' she said. 'The gazebo at two-thirty this afternoon.'

'Don't say anything to Candy,' he requested. '*Grazie*, it's good of you to agree—do you think she'll like the roses? They are the colour of her hair, are they not?'

Dominique couldn't help smiling a little. He really was a puzzle; he seemed to have an affection for Candice and yet at the same time, if Malina spoke the truth, he was seeing someone else. Would she learn who that person was when she kept her rendezvous with him?

'Roses have always been her favourite flower; I remember that she carried them at your—wedding. She sent me some lovely photographs of the two of you.'

'Yes, our wedding,' he murmured, his head bowed over the yellow roses. 'She looked so lovely, so full of life and laughter that day. The sun shone as we came out of the church and it was Presidio who took those photographs. He has an artistic eye, did you know that? I often think that had he not been the eldest son and born to the responsibility of the estate he would have taken to an artistic occupation. But the estate had need of him, especially when it became a co-operative, so he took the reins and has guided it into being one of the most successful ventures in southern Italy. Had the breaking up of the land into parcels happened in my father's time, he would have been horrified. He was of the old school, you understand. Very much the local squire, as you would call it in England. Alas, I don't remember him clearly, but Presidio sometimes talks of him—and our mother. He has their portraits in his den, have you seen them, Nicky?'

She shook her head. 'I've never been invited into your brother's den.'

'Is that so?' Tony raised an eyebrow and his likeness to Presidio was suddenly there. 'That must be remedied. He has some of his wood sculptures there and you would be interested——'

'Please, Tony,' she broke in, 'don't go implying to him that I would like to visit his den. I am only the nurse here, remember.'

'You are the sister of my wife——'

'The wife you are inclined to neglect,' she reminded him.

The look he gave Dominique was of self-reproach mixed with a certain pain. 'You are thinking that Candy has known very little happiness with me, eh? You are thinking that if I had a commitment here in San Sabina I should have kept away from your sister?'

'Yes,' she admitted, 'that's exactly what I'm thinking.'

'But then,' he shrugged slightly, 'you are an unselfish person, Nicky, and not all of us are made that way. Candice had such verve and gaiety and when we danced and were together nothing else seemed to matter. We got carried away—these things happen.'

'I know,' Dominique said in a gentler tone of voice.

'I'm not such a vinegar puss that I don't realise that feelings can overrule the sensible resolves we make for ourselves, and to be fair to you, Tony, I do happen to know that Candy led you to believe that she was pregnant. She loved you so much, you realise that?'

'*Si*, we all like to be loved,' he said rather sadly. 'We like it, but it can lead to complications that some of us are too hot-hearted to care about at the time. I have not the iron will of Presidio. I still wonder that he didn't strike me dead——'

Tony broke off, and Dominique gazed at him with startled eyes.

'Why should he want to do that, Tony? Surely not because you married Candice?'

'Ah no, you misunderstand! It relates to what I want to talk over with you later on—you will come to the gazebo?'

'Yes.' Her curiosity was very much aroused, and so was her apprehension. She had the feeling she was going to hear something very much to Candy's disadvantage.

'Tony, when you see Candy you'll notice a change in her. She'll tell you about it, and it's very important that you keep her buoyed up and don't let her down in any way.'

'Nicky?'

'She has started to walk again.'

'*Santo Dio!*' Something blazed in his eyes, then just as swiftly was blotted out . . . as the sun is when a cloud covers it. It was no superficial thing that was troubling him, and Dominique felt a sense of storm in the air.

'You saw her walk?' Tony searched Dominique's face. 'You were there when it happened?'

'Yes, I was very much there,' she said drily. 'Candy

will tell you all about it, so be glad for her——'

'Of course I'm glad for her.' His face darkened. 'What do you take me for—do you think I like to see her the way she has been?'

'Some men in your position might find it convenient,' Dominique said frankly, 'to have a wife who can't do anything but lie helpless while they carry on a liaison elsewhere. That's what you've been doing, isn't it? That's why you need to talk with me—you need to air your conscience?'

'No,' he exclaimed. 'It isn't like that——'

'You mean you love this other person and you care about Candy at the same time? Is that it, Tony? You do care about my sister?'

'Of course I care,' he groaned. 'I don't want to hurt her and I need you to tell me how I can avoid hurting her.'

'Tony, that's a lot to ask of me!' Dominique felt the apprehensive beat of her heart. 'If you have another emotional involvement then Candy is bound to be hurt. It can't be avoided, but I beg of you to avoid it until she's strong again and able to decide for herself what to do. You owe her that.'

'I know,' he said heavily. 'But I beg of you to let me talk about it—I must talk with someone and you—you are kind, Nicky. You have *simpatia* for those in trouble—and I am very greatly troubled.'

He looked so much like a hurt boy that Dominique's sympathy was aroused and she knew that if he didn't talk about this other involvement to her, then he might be driven to confide in Candice and it might set her back at this very delicate time when she needed the confidence to look forward to being vital and active again.

'We'll meet,' Dominique promised him. 'I'll listen

to what you have to say—just don't say it to Candy right now. She's on a tightrope taking careful steps, Tony. There's a long fall under her feet and no net to catch her if you unbalance her—you understand?'

'*Si*.' A grateful look stole into her eyes. 'I wish I could depend on you, Nicky.'

'Don't depend on me to help solve your problem,' she warned. 'I'm on Candy's side, candidly.'

'It's to be expected,' he agreed, 'but you are a fair-minded person and it will help me to talk with you. What is it you British say when someone needs to—to talk seriously?'

'To unburden one's soul.'

'Ah yes, from the time of the great Bard the British have found a way to express a thing with romantic exactitude. That is exactly what I wish to do, to unburden my soul.'

'Then I'll see you at two-thirty,' she promised. 'Candy will love the roses; they're the colour of hope and she needs all the hope she can get, Tony.'

'*Si*.' His face was like an Adonis mask, a dark sad look in the deep-set Latin eyes. '*Arrivederci*, Nicky.'

He went bounding up the stairs and she watched him a moment, her own eyes gravely grey, then she continued on her way to the kitchen to order her sister's lunch. There she had a cup of coffee with Cook and relaxed for a while as the large Italian woman rolled *pasta* and talked of her large family. A couple of her sons were working as waiters in London, and Dominique sat and listened and tried to stop worrying for a while about those two upstairs and what was to become of their relationship.

Would she end up taking Candice home with her to London? It would be such a pity. Italy was a warm-hearted country, picturesque and full of quaint customs. Especially here in San Sabina, uninvaded as yet by the sophistication of Rome. Here in the rural south the people still clung to their strong family ties; here in this very house it was evident that the Romanos brothers were linked by a strong affection.

She wondered what Tony had meant when he had said that it was a wonder Presidio had not struck him dead. Why should he say such a thing? What could have happened at some time to have alienated them? It must have been something serious, but it was in the past, if their present attitude towards one another was anything to go by.

Would he tell her about it when they met in the gazebo? He had said he would do so and she admitted frankly to herself that she wanted to hear everything that related to this other person in his life; this shadowy involvement which had caused a rift between him and his brother and was now affecting his marriage.

'The *signorina* looks worried,' Cook remarked. 'You have a troubled heart about your sister?'

'Yes,' Dominique sighed.

'But her health improves since you took charge of her.' Cook slapped a large expanse of pastry and expertly lined a dish with it. 'Her appetite has certainly improved and she eats the good food that I cook for her instead of playing about with it. I used to say that if she didn't wish to eat the food then she should at least not pick it to bits so I couldn't take it home to my Dino.'

Dominique smiled slightly, knowing Dino to be Cook's rather lazy husband who hung about the local cafés most of the day playing card games with his cronies.

Italian women, she had noticed, were very good at keeping the home going and being tolerant of menfolk who often had a roving eye and a disposition to match.

If this tendency to stray was in Tony, then Candice would have to adopt the Italian woman's attitude, or leave him. It would depend on how much she loved him, and it seemed to Dominique that if you loved a man with every bit of yourself, then it would be hell on earth to have to share him with somebody else.

The thought startled her, it was such a fierce one . . . and it was accompanied by an image not of Tony Romanos but of his brother Presidio. In her mind's eye she saw him vividly, lean, dark and arrogant as a centurion of old Rome, armoured to conquer, but never to be conquered himself.

In a dazed kind of way she watched Cook filling a pastry shell with tomatoes and anchovies, covering them with a thick layer of hot cheese flavoured with spice and chopped parsley.

The next moment a great slice of it was placed on a plate in front of her. 'There,' said Cook, 'eat and grow plump like an Italian girl and one of our handsome men will want to marry you!'

'Marriage to an Italian?' mocked a voice. 'She wouldn't know what to do with him! Had she the *sal* that makes a man dance attendance upon a woman she wouldn't talk of joining a nunnery!'

After the first shock of the words Dominique turned her head and met the malicious eyes of Malina, who had entered the kitchen just as Cook had spoken her jovial words. The contrast was like walking away from a cosy fire into a cold blast of snow that left a sting in the air.

'Eat your *pasta*,' Cook urged.

Dominique rose to her feet. 'I'll take it up with me on my sister's tray.'

Malina came to the table and watched as the tray

was prepared. All at once she met Dominique's eyes and they were coal-dark with animosity. 'I would suggest that the two of you go into a nunnery,' she said. 'Antonio doesn't want her, he has other fish to fry. I told her so—well, she asked, didn't she?'

Dominique picked up the tray and walked towards the door with it. Perhaps she was being melodramatic, but Malina wore one of those big-stoned Florentine rings which looked very much like an antique poison-ring, the compartment for the poison being under the large moonstone with which the ring was set. It gleamed on her dark-skinned hand like a malignant eye, just the sort of thing to appeal to this woman with her medieval looks and her smouldering jealousy where Tony was concerned.

'As I told you, Malina, if you ever harm my sister again I shall see to it that the police are informed. Ever since Tony brought her to this house she's been miserable and ill and I know you've had a hand in it. The Romanos brothers might think of you as loyal and devoted, but I think you're a mischief-maker. I think you'd like Tony all to yourself, but he's young and he thinks of you as his nanny.'

Malina's skin rarely showed any colour but Dominique's remark made her flush, it showed in her neck, beneath her eyes and high on her forehead where the black hair was drawn back. 'How dare you!' The words had a whispery sound. 'I shall report you to Don Presidio as insolent——'

'Go ahead and do so,' Dominique rejoined. 'I'm not a servant in this house, so I can't be dismissed out of hand because I refer to you as the nanny. It's what you are, isn't it? Even if you take it upon yourself to behave like a member of the Don's family.'

'I'll have you know——'

'And I'll have you know this,' Dominique stood there, tray in hand, her eyes meeting Malina's fearlessly. 'Don Presidio is my brother-in-law and I'll exert my rights if you dare to even enter my sister's room with your evil insinuations—and intentions. Tony is a grown-up man and he has no further need of a nanny to hold his hand. I would imagine that you have helped to make him unreliable and vacillating; by doing that you made yourself seem indispensable. No one is that, Malina. We can all be replaced one way or another, as you have taken pains to point out to Candice. Well, if it turns out that Tony wants someone else, then let him have her. My sister certainly has the *sal* to make a dozen men dance attendance upon her and I—I shan't be sorry to take her away from this house. A house is only warm and beautiful if there's love in it, but I've seen no evidence of that since I came to the Villa Dolorita!'

Having said her piece Dominique marched out of the kitchen with her sister's luncheon tray and almost collided with someone in the passage. 'Oh—mind!' she gasped.

'You mind, miss!' It was the Don, and he was glowering down darkly at Dominique. 'I heard every word you were shouting in there—what's the meaning of it?'

'If you heard me,' still in a fighting mood she met his eyes defiantly, 'then I've no need to explain, have I?'

'Meaning, miss, that you dislike my house?'

'Its architecture is faultless, *signore*, but apart from that——'

'You damned impudent girl!'

'May I pass, *signore*? My sister's lunch is getting cold.'

He stared down intently at her, his brows joined blackly. 'You're as white as a sheet—what's wrong?'

'Just about everything,' she said tensely. 'If your brother imagines that Candice is going to share him with someone else, then he'd better start thinking again. Candy is English, like me, and we have too much self-respect to go in for co-operative loving! Please, will you step aside?'

'Don't use that tone of voice to me, miss, and don't tell me to stand aside in my own house!'

'I'm well aware that it's your house, *signore*, but I was invited here to nurse your brother's wife and I would like her to have her lunch while it's still hot and tasty. You must admit that Italian dishes have a tendency to lose their appeal when they cool down.'

'And English dishes retain their appeal whether hot or cold?'

'Please——' Temper was cooling in her and she felt a vagrant sense of regret coming over her. She hadn't liked her own display of anger and the things she had said about the villa, but never had she disliked anyone as she disliked Malina; never had she known the urge to grab someone by the hair and yank it from the roots. That surge of primitive agitation had left her feeling ashamed and dejected. She hadn't lived up to Sister Superior's injunction that dignity in the face of fire was the true answer to all adversity ... as shown by the courageous Nurse Edith Cavell, one of Dominique's heroines.

'I can see that something has very much upset you.' The Don stood aside and gestured with his hand. 'We will talk about it later on.'

'I can't,' she said automatically. 'I've arranged to meet—I have to see someone else.'

'Someone else? Some—man?'

He said it as if he had some sort of claim upon her time and attention and a spark lit the dying fire in Dominique. 'Yes.' She gave him a defiant look. 'Have you any objection, Don Presidio, as to how I spend my free time, and with whom?'

She didn't know why she didn't simply tell him that she had been asked by his brother to offer some advice on a matter that was troubling him, but she was feeling perverse, and the hateful Malina had touched a sore which she had thought was healed. There was no man to whom she wanted to appeal, so what did it matter if she lacked *sal*, a Latin word for sensual warmth and excitement?

'I was not aware that you knew any of the local men,' said the Don coldly and very much on his dignity, a flare to his Latin nostrils.

'You would be unaware,' she rejoined, 'as like everyone else you take me for a plain dogsbody in a pair of glasses!'

'Dogsbody?' he exclaimed. 'What on earth is that?'

'A drudge and a doormat,' she said distinctly. 'Someone other people kick around and wipe their feet on, *signore*. I'm sure you would agree that the appellation suits someone as lacking in *sal* as I am!'

With that Dominique marched off with Candy's tray, head held high as she crossed the hall and mounted the stairs. 'Candy,' she prayed, 'hurry up and get well so we can both leave this house and get back to normality in England. I can do my nursing and you can go dancing and, for heaven's sake, don't get enraptured by another good-looking Italian. Make it an Englishman next time; have his babies and be moderately happy.'

When she entered her sister's room the yellow roses had been arranged so they caught the sun, and Candice was holding Tony's hand and gazing at him in a kind of bemusement. He looked relieved when Dominique came forward with the tray.

'Ah, your lunch, *carina*! You must eat every scrap of it, to please me.'

'Stay with me, Tony—please!' The blue eyes pleaded, but he caught at her hand, kissed it and made for the door.

'I have to shave, my pet.' He rubbed his chin ruefully. 'Presidio sent me off so early that I had no time to use a razor and we Italians grow our beards so quickly. You don't want me looking scruffy, do you?'

'I just want you,' Candice said softly. 'If you—want me.'

'Have I ever shown that I didn't want you, *carina mia*?' He stood in the doorway and though he smiled Dominique saw that sad little shadow in his eyes. 'Proceed to eat your lunch, there's a good girl, and I will return in a while to tuck you in for your afternoon nap.'

'Share my nap, Tony? I'm feeling so much stronger——'

'I would, my pet, but I have to see someone.' A flicker of desperation came into his eyes and Dominique came to his rescue.

She stood the little tray across Candy's lap. 'You need food and rest, my dear, if you're going to get really well. Be sensible and don't rush your fences.'

'You,' Candy cast a resentful look at Dominique, 'what would you know about the way I feel? You've never wanted to sleep with a man!'

Silence struck at the room like a clap of thunder, then as if in embarrassment Tony quickly departed, closing the door behind him.

'Oh, he's gone,' Candy wailed. 'Why did you have

to interrupt us—I don't want any lunch, take it away!'

She made a movement as if to push the laden tray off the *chaise-longue*, and Dominique said warningly: 'You do that, like a spoiled brat, and I'll leave this house today. I mean it, Candy. I'm beginning to feel that I've had just about enough of the whole lot of you! Why don't you grow up and start acting like a woman instead of an adolescent!'

Candy gazed at Dominique in open-mouthed astonishment. 'You can't leave me,' she said at last. 'You wouldn't——'

'Just try me, Candy. Just do to that tray what you were about to do and I pack my bag, call a cab and leave today. I'll carry on with my own life and leave you to carry on with yours as best you can. We're both adults, even if you choose to act like a fifteen-year-old, and you've had it proved to you that you can walk if you make the effort. You don't need me here, except as dogsbody. Someone to fetch and carry for you, and not mind when you feel like being insulting!'

'Nicky!' Candice looked amazed at her usually cool, collected and unobtrusive sister. 'I've never—never heard you speak like that.'

'Well, you've heard me now,' Dominique rejoined, and she didn't regret a word of her outburst. It had been boiling up in her, the way everyone took for granted that she was some kind of automaton who just stood by with soothing words and actions while other people had their traumas and showed their temperament. Candice would have swept that tray of food from the lounger and then watched with sulky satisfaction while Dominique cleared up the mess.

She drew a long, shaky breath. 'Are you going to eat your lunch, Candy, or shall I take the tray back to the kitchen? Please make up your mind.'

'Are you wild because of what I said?' Candice spoke in her little girl voice. 'I only said it, Nicky, because it's true—you aren't interested in men in that way.'

'If I were,' Dominique retorted, 'it would be my own business. Like everyone else you take it for granted that I'm of a different species—perhaps filled in with kapok from the waist downward!'

Candice gave a gasp which turned into a giggly laugh. 'Nicky, that's the naughtiest thing I ever heard you say!'

Dominique had flushed slightly at her own remark. 'It's probably the most relevant. Why should everyone assume that my feelings aren't as normal as theirs?'

'Because you're going to join St Anselma's.' Candice spooned melon into her mouth. 'Women who do that aren't really interested in men, are they? I mean, not in the sexy way. They're sort of frigid, aren't they?'

'Like me?' Dominique said drily. 'With my lack of looks it wouldn't do for me to be mad about men, would it?'

'You aren't pretty,' Candice said, perhaps a shade smugly. 'But your hair's nice, and when you take off those glasses your eyes are a lovely shade of grey and you have really long lashes—really long so you don't need to put mascara on them. If I'd been you, Nicky, I'd have got myself some contact lenses. I couldn't have borne to wear glasses. Men don't care for them. They make girls look—well, you know.'

'As if they might have a few brains?'

'Mmmm, this is gorgeous *pizza*.' Candice was busily eating the slice which Cook had cut for Dominique. 'Trust Presidio to have the best cook in San Sabina. Everything of the best for him! Well, you do have brains, Nicky. You passed all your nursing exams with flying colours and you know things that make me feel a real dunce. Some of the boys I used to bring home to the flat were scared to open their mouths in front of you; they used to say how efficient you looked. They couldn't believe that we were really sisters—oh, Nicky, don't leave me all alone here! You won't, will you? You didn't really mean what you said—did you?'

'Every word,' Dominique smiled slightly, 'at the time. It's unusual for me to lose my temper, but this seems to be one of those days when everyone feels like sticking pins in me.'

'Who?' Candice had picked up a lamb chop in her fingers and was busy nibbling it. 'Do tell!'

'I had a little contretemps with Malina.' Dominique forked a fat golden chip from her sister's plate and chewed it. 'I don't think her influence upon your husband has been a very good one. I think she has set out to make him dependent on her judgment rather than his own, and it must have really rattled her ego when he brought you home to the villa to become his bride. I can't make out why Don Presidio doesn't see through her. He's far more shrewd than Tony, but being Italian I suppose he's also sentimental where older women are concerned. Italians don't allow the older generation to be pushed on one side, do they?'

'They've very aware of their obligations,' Candice agreed. Then for a moment she stopped eating and gazed in front of her with unseeing blue eyes. 'I think that's how Tony has come to regard me, Nicky, as if I'm an obligation rather than a woman he still wants to—to make love to. When I look at him I still melt inside for him, but he—he kisses me too politely! Men don't do that when they care for you! I tell myself he's the way he is with me because of the way I am, but suppose when I start walking about he's still *polite*—what shall I do, Nicky?'

'Right now you'll finish your lunch,' Dominique said firmly. 'Let the future take care of itself—don't anticipate.'

'That's easy enough to say. It isn't easy to walk away from someone you love, Nicky.'

'I don't imagine it is, my dear. I just want you to build up your strength, so eat that other lamb chop and the rest of those lovely golden chips. I want to take a tray of empty dishes down to the kitchen today.'

'Nicky, dear Nicky, don't you ever get tired of being with sick people and having to encourage them to get well? Don't you ever long for—love?'

'I like being a nurse,' Dominique said with a tilt to her chin. 'It's a very satisfying when I see a sick person rallying and sitting up and getting interested in life again.'

'Is that all the satisfaction you're going to ask of life?' Candice studied her sister with a certain concern, running her gaze up and down her slim, blue-clad figure. 'I hate to think of you as a nun. It means that you'll never have a man to hold you and thrill you—it is thrilling, Nicky. It's like nothing else you ever imagined and I know I couldn't face life without all that mad, marvellous fun, all the closeness and the joy of it!'

'Of course not,' Dominique agreed. 'It's the way you're made; you have a warm and giving nature.'

'So have you,' Candice declared. 'You're my sister and we can't be all that different—how can you think of locking up your feelings? How can you do it, Nicky?'

'It's what I've decided to do——'

'But you haven't made a firm commitment—you're still free to change your mind.'

'I don't want to change it.'

'I don't believe you!'

'You're going to have to believe it, Candy.'

'Oh, Nicky, haven't you ever felt *anything* for a man? Haven't you ever had a crush on a doctor?'

'Hardly.' Dominique broke into a smile. 'Contrary to what the magazine serials would have women believe, doctors and surgeons are busy men committed to their careers rather than chasing pretty nurses all over the hospitals. I've never seen much of that kind of thing. It would hardly do, would it, with people lying there dependent on our skills?' -

'You mean your heart has never skipped a beat for anyone? That your legs have never gone weak when a man has come near you and looked right into your eyes with that look which says, "I could take you, here and now, and your screams wouldn't stop me!" That's never happened to you, Nicky?'

Dominique hesitated for half a heartbeat. 'No,' she said, and she knew she told a lie that mocked her through the chambers of her mind and deep inside her where she had submerged the girl of seventeen and eighteen who like other girls had dreamed of a romantic lover who would sweep her off her feet and adore her even if she wasn't beguilingly pretty like her sister.

'Haven't you ever wanted it to happen?' Candice persisted.

'Not since I grew up and became sensible.'

'Sensible?' Candice pulled a face. 'Ugh, what a word! Who wants to go through life being sensible? It sounds like flat shoes, baggy skirts and your hair in a bun!'

'Well, being sensible makes sense for me. Now finish off that fruit salad and I can take the tray away and make you nice and comfortable for your nap.'

'Nicky, do stop using those old-maidish expressions,' Candice begged as she chased a cube of pineapple around the fruit bowl.

'I am an old maid, sister dear,' Dominique reminded her.

'You're only two years older than me.' Candice gave her an exasperated look. 'I'm beginning to wonder if you're scared stiff of men—is that it?'

'I don't think so.' Dominique broke into a smile. 'It's probably the other way around, you said yourself that your boy-friends found me off-putting.'

'Oh, they were boys. I'm talking about men—men like Presidio, for example. What do you think of him, Nicky, seriously? I don't see how you couldn't have noticed him—does he scare you?'

'Heavens, no!' Even to her own ears the denial sounded a little too high-toned. 'Why on earth should he—a mere man?'

'Come off it, Nicky, there's nothing mere about the Don of San Sabina. A little bird whispered to me that you had dinner alone with him the other evening, out on the *corte* under the myrtles. He can be darned attractive and attentive when he's in the mood; was he in that mood the other evening out there under the myrtles and the stars?'

'Not particularly.' Dominique spoke in her coolest voice and, as if she were in Matron's office, curled her toes in her nursing shoes so the tension in the rest of her body wouldn't reveal itself. It was a trick imparted to her by an actress she had nursed; it might cramp her instep, she had been told, but it wouldn't cramp her style. Right now (and she was inwardly appalled that it was so) she needed to act in front of her sister as if the mere mention of Presidio Romanos left her cool and contained.

'What did you talk about?' Candice wanted to know, an inquisitive gleam in her blue eyes. 'And why didn't you tell me you had dinner alone with him?'

'I probably forgot all about it,' Dominique returned airily, with knotted toes. 'He was just being polite when he asked me to dine with him; he probably felt sorry for your old maid sister and·thought he had a duty to put up with my company for an hour or so. The food was excellent, but I forget most of the conversation. I don't suppose it was very sparkling.'

'You're being very cool about him.' Candice gave Dominique a suspicious look. 'He's extremely eligible, you know.'

'And extremely Italian. Even if he were interested in marriage and I had your flirtatious nature, his eligibility wouldn't do me a scrap of good. I haven't got what it takes to arouse romance in Don Presidio, nor do I wish to have it. He has set his course, Candy, and mine is set, so don't go getting any matchmaking ideas. They'd make me want to crawl into a hole out of his way; I'd be too embarrassed to face him. It sticks in his throat that his brother married an English girl, so it's ludicrous to suggest that it meant something because I had a meal with him. I was there, and I can assure you it was a relief to both of us when we said goodnight.'

'So much for the stars and the myrtles.' Candice looked perplexed by her sister's lack of interest in leading a man on. 'So you just ate, made small talk, and then went to bed?'

'*I* went to bed,' Dominique said tartly. 'He may have sat up to midnight going over his accounts for all I care. The next thing I knew he was waking me up to tell me you were sick; that's probably why having dinner with him slipped my mind and why I failed to mention such a great event to you.'

'I suppose so.' Candice drew her bottom lip between

her teeth. 'I—I thought I was going to die—I couldn't eat another prawn if someone offered me a diamond to go with it. Ugh, the very thought of that night——'

'Don't think about it, it's over and done with.' Dominique lifted the tray from her sister's lap and set it on one side. 'How about trying a few steps to the bathroom?'

'No—I'll fall——'

'I'll be holding you, Candy, and this time we needn't be scared that the tide is going to sweep us out to sea. Do try.'

'Dare I?' Candice looked half eager, half reluctant.

'You used to be very daring. Nothing frightened you, Candy.'

'All right, then.' Candice pushed aside the light covering and with Dominique's help she stood up, only to fold at the ankles and sag with a cry. 'I can't do it—God, it's like walking on jelly!'

'You can do it,' Dominique insisted. 'What a person has done once a person can do again and if I can't hold you and you fall, you have a nice soft carpet to fall down on instead of rough stone steps. Make the effort, Candy dear. Those ankles of yours are too pretty not to be used.'

'W-what a bully you can be, Nicky!' Candice stumbled forward. 'Are you l-like this with all your p-patients?'

'Yes, I'm a holy terror—there, you're making it, you brave girl! We're almost into the bathroom, that's it, just a few more steps ... hurray, wonderful!' Dominique hugged her sister and when they kissed their lips felt each other's wet cheeks. Laughing and crying, they clung together ... for the moment Dominique had forgotten that she was meeting Tony Romanos clandestinely so he could tell her about the other girl in his life.

For now Dominique didn't want to think of anything but the blessed joy of sharing Candy's discovery that her body was mobile again.

'I can walk,' Candice said breathlessly. 'Oh, isn't it wonderful, Nicky! Now Tony will want me again—he will, won't he?'

'Of course he will,' Dominique assured her ... knowing in her heart that she was very unsure of her sister's Italian husband.

CHAPTER SEVEN

IT rained that afternoon and Dominique hurried to the gazebo beneath the wide brim of an umbrella she had found in a cupboard near the kitchen; she wore her nurse's cape over her blue dress.

There had been a hint of storm in the weather all day, so she wasn't surprised by the rain. Somehow it seemed appropriate; the sun shouldn't shine when a person was on their way to hear some bad news. She felt certain that Tony was going to tell her something that would affect her sister's life, and she felt animosity towards him as she came in sight of the stone gazebo, with its peaked roof, set there among the trees like a gnome's dwelling.

She entered, folded the umbrella and shook it outside the doorway. She was first to arrive and was glad of that. It would give her a chance to gather her composure much like the cape that was gathered about her slim body against the rainy chill in the usually warm air of San Sabina. If Tony Romanos was going to let her sister down, then Candice was going to need all the strength which Dominique could muster on her behalf.

Today Candice had walked and nobody was going to make an invalid of her again. Dominique was resolved upon that, and she stood there in the doorway of the gazebo, ready to defend her sister like a tigress which had licked a cub to its struggling feet.

Love might be a wonderful thing—if it was reciprocated. But it seemed to Dominique that love was a bitter honey and best left alone if the loved one felt only pity instead of passion. She had glimpsed pity in the Latin eyes of her sister's husband, and if that was all he had left for Candice, then it would be better for them to part. The thing that Dominique dreaded was that he was going to ask her to tell Candice that he wanted to set her aside for someone he loved more.

Oh God, how was she going to do it? She had battled to get Candy back on her feet and now she felt so weary that she could feel her own legs trembling. Then as Tony's lean dark figure emerged from among the trees she felt her heart pounding with apprehension. As he drew nearer to the gazebo she could see the gravity of his expression, his black hair soaked with the rain, drops of it running down his face and soaking into the raised collar of his jacket.

'You came!' He hastened into the gazebo and thrust the wet hair back from his eyes. 'I am grateful, Nicky.'

'You're awfully wet, Tony——' She felt constrained all at once; she didn't want to hear about some intimacy in his life which excluded Candice and she wanted to tell him so.

'I shall soon dry off,' he said. 'I didn't look in on Candy because I didn't want to be delayed. She ate a good lunch?'

'A very good one.' Dominique watched him warily as he shook the rain from his jacket and began to pace back and forth.

'Good,' he said abstractedly. 'Ah, how do I begin— I had the words all in order and now they are all over the place again.'

'There is only one place to begin, Tony.' Let him get it over with, she told herself. If he had to discuss the matter then it was better at the present time if he discussed it with her; better that she act as a buffer before it became necessary for Candy to be told that he didn't want her, he wanted someone else.

'I hope you aren't going to be shocked by what I have to tell you,' he said, coming to a standstill in front of her. 'I'm afraid it isn't a very pretty story.'

'I didn't expect it to be, Tony.' She met his eyes unsmilingly. He looked wretched and unhappy, but she had no sympathy to offer him. 'Just tell me about it in plain words; I'll listen, but I can't promise you a solution, and as I said before, I'm on my sister's side and it's her wellbeing I have to consider—not yours.'

'*Si*, it is natural you should feel that way, but don't steel yourself against me, Nicky. Try to understand that men and women can be carried away by their feelings; that not all of us have your kind of discipline. I admire you for it.'

'Don't admire me for something I was never called upon to resist. No one ever tempted me to stray from the path of duty, Tony, so I shan't be self-righteous because you've strayed.' She gazed into his eyes steadily. 'I just wanted you to know that if I'm biased it's because Candice is my sister, all the family I have. I'm here right now because I want things sorted out for her sake—I don't want her hurt too much. She's been hurt enough.'

He inclined his head and a spasm of pain went across his face. 'I should not have married her, that's what you're thinking?'

'I know it was difficult for you, Tony. I know she lied to you, but we've gone all over that. Now you'd better tell me your story.'

'Yes,' he sighed. 'Won't you sit down? I think that seat is quite dry; this is a strong little building and the rain doesn't come in, only a few moths and spiders, and I'm sure you don't mind those, eh?'

'Not too much,' she agreed, and taking a Kleenex from the pocket of her cape she gave the stone bench a rub with it and it was a relief to sit down. She felt so keyed up that she could feel her legs trembling under her; get it over, she wanted to beg of him. Instinct warned her that she was in for a shock.

'It began years ago,' he said, leaning there against the wall, the dark wet hair in jags against his forehead, his eyes brooding in his lean face. 'I was not yet eighteen and when this girl and I clapped eyes on each other it was, if I may use a cliché, as if Romeo saw Juliet for the first time—a meeting that was to be as fateful as theirs. It isn't usual in Italy for the women to have very fair hair, but this girl had such hair, and it was long and braided around her head in a rather quaint fashion. In contrast her eyes were a dark honey colour and her lips were red and rather full. She seemed the loveliest thing I had ever looked upon and when she looked at me I knew she felt attracted to me. We seemed meant for each other, but she was engaged to marry another man—that man was my brother Presidio.'

'Oh no!' the words escaped Dominique before she could stop them.

'Oh yes,' Tony agreed. 'You see the problem right

away, don't you? This lovely young girl was going to marry my brother and it was me to whom she was drawn. It couldn't be otherwise, somehow. She was my age and I saw in her my temperament rather than that of Presidio, who even then was bound up in his work. The marriage, you see, had been arranged many years before when my parents were still alive. Presidio would honour the arrangement because that was his way, but it didn't allow for the fact that women and men have feelings which aren't always honourable, and Amatrice and I—well, the outcome was as you can imagine.'

'Can I?' Dominique's voice was quiet enough, but inwardly she was seething. So this was what she must sit here and listen to, the seduction of the Don's bride-to-be by his young brother! She was shocked; not only shocked but strangely hurt by such a betrayal. Perhaps everyone was right about her; perhaps she did lack an understanding of the desires and passions that could tear loyalties apart and wreck lives. She knew just by looking at Tony that those things had happened here at the Villa Dolorita and parts of the wreckage still clung to the lives of the Romanos brothers.

'We couldn't help ourselves.' Tony spoke low and painfully. 'We used to meet in secret and at first we only talked together. Amatrice was staying with an aunt in San Sabina, though she came from another part of Italy——'

'Vicovaro, the place of lovely women,' Dominique interposed quietly.

'Ah, how did you know that?' Tony exclaimed.

'Your brother mentioned it.'

'You mean—he talked to you of Amatrice? He told you——?'

'No.' She shook her head. 'He only mentioned that

she was extremely pretty and he said she came from Vicovaro.'

'He said no more than that? He made no mention of me?'

'No, Tony. I rather doubt if Don Presidio could be disloyal to a member of his family.'

'Ah!' Tony groaned and a flush swept to the roots of his hair. 'I didn't realise that you could hit below the belt, Nicky.'

'Perhaps you don't know me very well,' she rejoined. 'It wasn't a very nice thing for you to do, was it? Seducing your brother's *fidanzata*?'

His flush of shame lingered and he dropped his gaze like a shamefaced boy.

Always, she thought, there would be something of the boy about Tony Romanos. Perhaps that was why women fell in love with him . . . Dominique gazed at him dispassionately and knew that he couldn't move her heart. She saw beneath his good looks the flaw of weakness in his character; he was not made of the same material as his brother.

'We were very young, Amatrice and I,' he said. 'I know it's a poor excuse for the way we behaved, but she needed affection and attention and Presidio seemed always tied up at business meetings. Then I had to go to university and Amatrice and I said goodbye to each other and she promised to write to me.'

Tony paused and gazed sombrely out of the doorway of the gazebo, and all at once it hit Dominique that it was here in this little stone garden house that he used to meet his brother's girl. It was here they used to kiss and whisper together; here that they had said goodbye.

'What happened to her, Tony?' Dominique could feel the almost apprehensive beating of her own heart.

'She had my baby,' he said slowly. 'Presidio never

told me and I think he stopped her from doing so. He thought it would ruin my life if I was saddled with a wife and child at the age of eighteen; he can be a very hard man if a just one, Nicky, and he saw to it that Amatrice had every care, though he refused to marry her himself. She went into premature labour at her aunt's and, poor pretty Amatrice, she died at dawn giving birth to my daughter.

'Yes, I have a daughter, Nicky. She is eight years old and I go frequently to visit her. I know that you and Candy believed that my visits were to a woman, isn't that so?'

'Yes.' Dominique was gazing at him astounded. 'Why, Tony, doesn't the child live here at the villa with you?'

'Because she resides in a home for the mentally retarded,' he said draggingly. He swung round to look at Dominique and his eyes were ablaze with pain. 'It wasn't enough that Amatrice should die, the little girl had to be born that way. It seemed that Amatrice's labour dragged on and on and her aunt thought she could deal with the matter—when a doctor was eventually called in and the birth was induced, the child had suffered brain damage. Ah, but she's so beautiful to look at, Nicky, so much like her mother, but she will never be more than a child and it's estimated that her life span won't be a long one. I—I love her so——'

Suddenly, chilling Dominique through and through, he broke down and started to weep. In an instant Dominique was on her feet and across the gazebo and she had pulled his head down to her shoulder, her arms wrapped around him.

'Don't upset yourself so,' she murmured. 'These things happen and it's sad and terrible, but such children are so lovable and they accept love so readily. I'm sure you have found this to be so?'

'*Si.*' He drew a ragged breath. 'She knows me and flies into my arms when I go to see her, but when I'm not there—ah, Nicky, they tell me that she sits and mopes when I'm not with her and I—I want to bring her home to live with me, but how can I do it? There is Candy—there is Presidio—ah, tell me, please tell me what I should do?'

Dominique, who had worked for a while among retarded children, realised his dilemma and could no longer deny him her sympathy. Poor boy, he had certainly suffered for his wrongdoing, and so had that poor pretty girl who had been meant for Presidio. She didn't blame the Don for being unable to marry her after finding out that she and his young brother had been lovers, but it might have been the wisest course to have informed Tony of the girl's pregnancy and permitted them to marry. It might have saddled a mere boy with a wife and child, but it might have been the saving of Amatrice and their child might not have been born with a defect.

'Tony,' she said quietly, 'you must tell Candice what you've told me.'

'No,' he shook his head, 'she will turn against me. She is much like Amatrice, don't you see? She likes affection and attention, and more than once she has begged me for a child and I've denied her. At the time I thought her pregnant I was in terror that another child would be born like Rosalia and I couldn't bear the thought——'

'Your daughter was born that way because she suffered the injury during the over-long labour that her mother went into. Had that not happened, Tony, she would have been perfectly normal.'

'How can I be sure of that?' A tear edged its

way down his cheek.

'I'm sure the doctor said as much, and I'm certain the staff at the home have told you so. Haven't they?'

'Yes,' he agreed. 'You tell me to tell Candy—do you truly think she would understand? She's so young herself and she has been ill——'

'An illness brought on by those poisonous letters someone sent her,' Dominique reminded him. 'Don't you see, she believes you love someone else, and that's at the bottom of her trouble. She cares for you so much and when you absent yourself from the house, she doesn't know that you go to see a little girl—least of all your own little girl. You must tell her about Rosalia— for both your sakes.'

'Would you tell her for me?' he pleaded.

'No,' Dominique said firmly. 'You mustn't always hide behind other people, Tony. I feel certain that Candice will understand and want to care for Rosalia as much as you do. I know that my sister seems very young and clinging, but it's because most people have spoilt her and she needs to have something in her life that will make her realise that life isn't all dancing and dressing up and being the belle of the ball.'

'You can say that about your own sister?' Tony exclaimed in astonishment.

'It's the truth, Tony. You have said that she reminds you of Amatrice—wasn't Amatrice something of a butterfly, dipping her wings in the sunlight and unaware that she was doing wrong by flirting with you when she was engaged to your brother? No doubt you blame yourself for everything that happened, but love isn't made and a child isn't born unless a woman goes halfway to meet a man. Your brother realised that after he discovered her betrayal of his trust, that's why he couldn't marry her. He might have thought that she would one day be unfaithful to you; that it was in her nature to be faithless.

'You have to remember, Tony, that your brother was educated by the Jesuits, whereas he saw to it that you went to less restricting schools. He had been raised to draw a very definite distinction between right and wrong and so his judgments, at times, would seem harsh. I expect he has suffered because of the way your daughter was born—I wouldn't be in any doubt of that.'

'Wouldn't you?' he said broodingly. 'He has never suggested that I bring Rosalia to live at the villa.'

'Have you never asked him?'

'How would I dare?'

'Had you dared to ask, you might have found him only too willing to welcome the child. You never asked, so perhaps he thought you preferred that she be raised at the home.'

'Perhaps so.' He lifted his shoulders and sighed. 'She looks so much like Amatrice, the same shade of hair and eyes, and I have been reluctant to discuss the matter with him in case he couldn't endure to have under his roof the love-child of a girl he was to have married. There is much pride in Presidio.'

'I think there is charity in him as well,' Dominique murmured. 'Anyway, the most important thing is that you be candid with Candice. She needs to be told that it isn't another woman who takes you from her side but a small girl who needs love—the love of a father.'

'You really think that she'll understand—and forgive?' he asked, and as he spoke his hands gripped Dominique's shoulders and he gazed at her with eyes which had come alive. 'You don't think that she'll be disgusted with me?'

'She might feel rather let down, Tony, that you

aren't the shining young god she took you for, but I'm certain she loves you very much and wants above all to be assured that you love her. You do, don't you? You have got over what you felt for Amatrice?'

'Long ago,' he admitted. 'I would certainly have married her had I been told of her condition, but Presidio forbade her to write to me. His plan was that her child be adopted and then he would have returned her to her family, a girl estranged from her fiancé rather than an unmarried mother. But things didn't work out that way——'

'How did you come to learn of the baby?' Dominique asked. 'Did your brother tell you that Amatrice had died having a child?'

'No.' He shook his head. 'It was Malina who told me, and I was shocked and horrified, and furious with Presidio for keeping me in ignorance. We had a terrible fight, but eventually we came to terms over the matter and he understood my need to keep in touch with Rosalia. She was in that home because of me and I couldn't just leave her there and forget all about her. Sometimes I take her to the circus; she loves the clowns and the elephants, and I take her for drives and we have ice-cream and cake. Just to look at she seems perfectly normal, but she is mute and totally deaf and that's why she adores the clowns, because she can understand their mime and their antics. Ah, if Candice would take to her and want to mother her, but how can I be sure? Candy wants children of her own and she may not want my child by another woman.'

'It's true, Tony, she may not,' Dominique agreed. 'But you must be frank with her and tell her everything that you've told me.'

'Are you shocked, Nicky?' he wanted to know, and

still he held her by the shoulders as if he couldn't bear to let go of her sympathy. It showed in her eyes, how moved she was by the story of the little girl who was mute and who loved the clowns and was probably mystified to have a papa with whom she didn't live.

'When you become a nurse,' she said, 'you become shock-proof the first week you go on the wards. Life seems full of rules, but people manage to break most of them, don't they?'

'Have you broken many?' He smiled slightly as if he couldn't quite believe that she had.

'A few petty ones, but don't go taping me as a prig, Tony. The kind of temptations put in the way of pretty girls aren't put in the way of plain girls like me, so I'm not going to judge you or Amatrice—or even your brother for finding her behaviour unforgivable.'

Dominique paused and looked thoughtful. 'Perhaps he didn't love her enough—or did he love her too much?'

'Who knows?' Tony shrugged. 'I have never quite fathomed him; we are brothers but we have different natures—just as you and Candice have. If a man were married to you, Nicky, he wouldn't have to wonder if you would accept his mute child, would he? Charity shines out of your eyes.'

'No doubt,' she said drily. 'I'm a very dull and dutiful person, and it didn't always please me that Candice got all the icing while I was less scrumptious to look at. The Owl and the Pussycat, that's what the children at the convent used to call us. I always had my head in a book while Candy was busy charming everyone— you charmed her, Tony, and won her love, and you're going to have to find out if that love will be big enough to make room for Rosalia. If it isn't, what will you do? Who will you choose?'

'I don't want it to come to that,' he groaned. 'I want both of them, but I—I don't know what I'll do if Candy refuses to share our life with Rosalia. Nicky, would it not be better if you talked to her and made her see how much I care for her and for my *bambina*? Please, do this one last thing for me and tell her in your quiet way so she won't get all worked up—the way she did over the pearls. I couldn't stand another scene like that one! It got so out of hand—the two of us lost our tempers and the next thing I knew she had fallen down those steps and I thought she had broken her neck.'

Unaware in his emotional state, he was gripping Dominique until she felt that his fingers would break her collarbone. 'Tony——'

'Please,' he said hoarsely. 'I am at my wits' end. Candy isn't like you—you have a calmness in you and you see reason, but I know that if I try to talk to her it will all go wrong. When you love someone—I don't know why it is, but the emotions seem to get out of control and before you know where you are you are saying all the wrong things instead of the right ones. It is a delicate matter, you agree?'

'Yes,' Dominique sighed. It did seem that people in love had a tendency to distrust their own emotions, as if they lived too close to the centre of their own fire and were in constant danger from the very flames which were generated by their feelings for each other.

Love, it seemed, could be ecstasy or torment, but it could never be cosy.

'So I am to plead your cause,' she said, her gaze upon Tony's tormented face. 'It will only do half the work and you will still have to face each other and from that moment onward you'll have to work things out between you. I won't always be here——'

'Don't go away too soon.' In his anxiety, in his need to have her as his ally, Tony pulled her suddenly close to him, and it was at that crucial moment that a voice said, harshly:

'Are you up to your old tricks, brother? Are you using the gazebo for another of your damnable affairs?'

In a kind of startled reflex Tony seemed to press Dominique closer to him, and in stricken silence she seemed to let it happen.

'Let go of the girl,' the voice was low and deadly, 'unless you want me to break every lecherous bone in your body!'

Suddenly, violently, Tony swung round to face his brother, and in an instant the atmosphere in the gazebo was one of stark danger. Never in her life had Dominique sensed it so acutely ... it was as if the two men were going to leap at each other's throats, and as if to stop this she flung herself between them and thrust a hand against Don Presidio's chest.

'Don't!' she cried out.

'Get away!' He pushed her to one side and she stumbled ... this seemed to infuriate Tony all the more and he swung a wild punch which his brother parried, returning it with a driving, hate-filled blow that sent Tony sprawling on the ground, blood spilling from a cut lip. Instantly he was on his feet, spitting blood and cursing.

They fought while Dominique stood there in a kind of horrified daze. Their animal grunts and the thud of the blows made her want to scream.

'Stop it—are you both mad?' Again it was Presidio whom she tried to stop, and this time she got in the way of his swinging fist ... with terrible force it struck her on the side of the jaw and sent her spinning. She

couldn't save herself and went down with a thud that
shook her entire body, the pain seemed to explode in
her head and though she knew she had hit the floor
she could still feel herself falling . . . falling into a dark
pit filled with disconnected sounds she couldn't put
together.

'*Santo Dio!*' Hands gathered hold of her and
suddenly she was floating in the air . . . and then there
was nothing. Her head lolled and she hung limp as a
rag doll in the arms of Presidio Romanos.

Dominique came to with a splitting headache, a sore
face and a parched throat.

As she awoke with a groan, someone raised her head
and the brim of a glass was placed at her lips. The cool
tang of orange juice touched her lips and she drank
greedily from the glass, feeling the juice slide cool and
welcome down her dry throat.

Feeling revived, she raised her eyes to the person
who was assisting her to sit up and drink the delicious
juice. It came as something of a shock to meet the eyes
of Don Presidio whose fist had dealt her such a stunning blow.

They looked at each other and he seemed lost for
words . . . Dominique's jaw felt twice its size and she
carefully explored the inside area with her tongue. She
winced at the soreness and heard the Don mutter an
Italian imprecation to himself; a rather fierce one, for
she knew the language quite well by now.

'The girl is fetching some ice-water,' he said. 'Your
face will feel a little easier after it's been bathed—it
hurts, eh?'

She nodded and he eased her back against the pillows.

'Do you think you need a doctor?' He looked at her

with real concern in his eyes. '*Dio mio*, when you went down I thought I had killed you—why did you have to get in the way like that, eh? Talk of angels rushing in——'

'You two,' she mumbled, and it really hurt to talk, 'were intent on killing each other.'

'Possibly.' His lip twitched and she noticed some bruising on his face where Tony's fist had landed. 'It was seeing him there with you—you know about Amatrice, eh?'

'Yes, a-and about the little girl.'

'Ah yes, the child.' His face grew very sombre and remained that way all the time he bathed Dominique's face from the bowl of ice-water. The throbbing began to subside a little, but she felt curiously languid and lay there after he had carefully wiped her face with a towel.

'Does that feel easier?' As he spoke he brushed the hair away from her eyes. 'That was very foolhardy, what you did, Dominique, my fist could have smashed your glasses and hurt your eyes.'

'Where are my glasses——?'

'You don't need them right now.'

'I—I can never see too clearly without them.'

'It was I who was not seeing clearly, but Tony had hold of you and I could only think that history was repeating itself.'

'Amatrice was pretty, *signore*. I'd hardly appeal to your brother in that way—he was asking my advice about his child, he wants Candice to accept her. And he wants you to do the same, but of course it's difficult for you. She'd be a constant reminder of what happened, especially as she resembles her mother.'

In unsmiling silence the Don gazed at Dominique. 'You believe that is why I've never suggested that he have the child here?'

'Isn't it, *signore*?' He still sat quite close to her on the side of her bed and as she looked up at him she felt defenceless, loomed over by the span of his shoulders, by his Italian darkness and the memories she saw smouldering in his eyes.

'It would be natural—if you felt that way,' she added.

'Natural?' His black brows came together above his eyes. 'You think my poor damned heart would break all over again, is that it?'

'Y-you were going to marry Amatrice and she——'

'She let my brother make love to her, eh?'

'It would be a blow to your pride.'

'Only to my pride?'

'And to your other feelings——'

'And what kind of feelings are those, *signorina*?' He leaned a little closer, supported upon his arms at either side of Dominique so that he made her feel even more-helpless.

'You were going to marry her, s-so you must have—loved her.'

'What a romantic supposition, Nurse, especially from someone who informed me that I was against my brother marrying your sister because the marriage hadn't been arranged in the Italian way. At the time you said it I didn't get the impression that you thought arranged marriages were romantic, so what suddenly gives you the idea that I was madly enamoured of my bride-to-be?'

'You—you never bothered about finding someone to take her place.' Dominique edged her tongue around her swollen lips. 'M-may I have a drink of orange juice, my mouth feels so sore?'

'*Demonio*,' he growled, raising himself and reaching

for the glass. Ice tinkled in the jug of juice as he refilled the glass.

'Come!' He lifted her, his arm firm and strong about her body that felt so fragile as he held her. 'By the saints, you feel as if you might break in half—replace her, you say? Replace that harlot?'

The words went through Dominique as if tipped with steel. As she sipped the juice she couldn't look away from him, it was if he mesmerised her with his bitter cynicism.

'I'm sorry,' she murmured.

'Sorry?' He frowned darkly. 'It would have been worse had I married her before she was unfaithful, wouldn't you say?'

'I expect it would. Thank you, I've had enough.'

As he set the glass aside his lip took a slight twist. 'Enough of all of us, I think. When you took on the task of nursing your sister you didn't quite expect to get embroiled in a family dispute, did you? I recall that you asked to be treated as a nurse rather than a relation by marriage, but our decisions and desires are often taken out of our hands and we feel some other force at work, taking hold of us and pulling us in a direction we didn't dream of. That is the way of life. It won't always be arranged—you see that?'

'Yes, *signore*.'

'And so you are drawn into our family disgrace and you tell me that Tony wants to be a full-time father to the child?'

'Yes. He's very sincere about it and he obviously cares about her. But he doesn't want to upset Candice—or you.'

'A pity he didn't take the same view before he brought about her birth,' the Don rejoined, his mouth hard and cynical. 'He played the philanderer and the girl involved died because he couldn't keep his hands to himself. She died and that *poverina* was born—he told you that she is mute and will remain childlike?'

'Yes, he told me everything.'

'Were you shocked?'

'I was sorry for you all.'

'That's very charitable of you, Dominique.' Again his lip twisted. 'I should have thought that with your views on life you would have felt inclined to condemn my brother's behaviour, not to mention the girl's.'

'I hope I'm not that narrow-minded,' Dominique protested, feeling a stab of hurt inside her. 'They were young and they allowed their foolish hearts to rule them. It could happen to anyone——'

'To you, do you think?'

She flushed and her face stung from the bruising he had inflicted. 'You don't have to be sarcastic—I've taken enough from you w-without that——'

'You always accuse me of being sarcastic towards you.'

'Because you are.' She gave him an indignant look. 'Because one woman didn't turn out to be angelic you take it out on others. It isn't my fault that Amatrice betrayed you—according to what Tony told me, you were always minding your business and you didn't show her a lot of attention; being young she could have thought that you didn't love her, so she turned to someone else for the affection she craved.'

'Quite the little philosopher, aren't you, Nurse? Did they teach you that at the convent, or was it part of your medical training?'

'Oh——' She turned her head away from him and laid the unhurt side of her face in the pillow. 'I'm too tired to argue with you—you always think you know best, and that's why Tony asked me for a little advice.

I don't pretend to know the answers; I warned him that Candice may object to being a mother to his love child.'

'Because Candice isn't like you, eh? You'd take on a man's love child, would you?'

'I expect I would,' she said wearily. 'Nobody loves me, *signore*, so I expect I understand the need for it. Candice needs only to look the way she does for some man to care about her and if she breaks up with your brother, there will be someone else to desire her.'

'Is that what you really think?' Suddenly the Don's warm hands were upon Dominique's shoulders and he was lifting her from the pillows so she hung in his grasp, the fair hair tousled about her face, pale but for the livid swelling where he had struck her.

'Well?' He gave her a slight shake. 'Answer me!'

'I—I usually say what I mean.'

'*Santo Dio*, spare me the pathos!' His teeth seemed to bite on the words so they had an edge to them. 'There's more going on inside you than will ever go on inside that candyfloss sister of yours, so stop all this nonsense about being the daisy by the wayside while she enjoys the passions of the tropical flower! She's just another pretty blonde who thinks every man owes her his adulation. When Tony showed her that his adulation was divided she took to that damn bed and became an hysterical paralytic. You know it, so admit it—come on!'

'Y-you're hurting me,' Dominique protested, tears filling her eyes. 'You seem to get p-pleasure out of hurting me——'

'I'll get pleasure out of strangling you if you don't admit that I'm right,' he said through gritted teeth.

'Oh, leave me alone——' She gave him some weak resistance and felt the tears tumble down her cheeks.

It wasn't like her to cry in front of anyone, least of all this arrogant man, but why did everyone use her when they wanted to release their feelings? 'I'm a person, too,' she cried. 'I have feelings, but no one ever seems to think that my feelings count!'

'Well, that little outcry proves something, Nurse. It proves that you haven't flesh of ice.' He watched her tears as if it satisfied him to see her dissolving from cool efficiency into limp, tear-wet misery. He let the storm have its way with her; allowed it to sweep over her until her sobs grew less racking and finally abated, leaving her so listless that when he laid her down, wiped her face and covered her up, she was already half asleep.

'*Dolce reposa*.' He was turning away from the bed when in the voice of a child who believed she was back at the convent Dominique said clearly:

'It's so cold and dark—oh, Daddy, don't go away, please!'

The Don stood there, tall and brooding in the dusky room. A clock ticked and through the open window drifted a sound of seabirds and the splash of the evening tide as the waves hit the shore.

Dominique didn't awake as she was drawn into a pair of strong arms and cradled against those first lonely nights when Peter Davis had returned to the East and left his young daughters with the nuns. The dream and the reality merged into one and with a soft sigh Dominique settled into the masculine arms.

'Daddy, you didn't go away?'

'No, my child.'

'I'm so glad.'

She slept, deep and warm in the arms of Presidio Romanos.

CHAPTER EIGHT

DOMINIQUE took the letter down to the beach and read it yet again, dwelling in shocked disbelief upon the passage which asked her to admit or deny that she had been conducting an immoral association with the man who employed her as a nurse in his household.

The letter came from the House of St Anselma.

She let it fall to the sands and pressed her hand to the side of her face; her mind raced with questions and suddenly an answer came and she no longer doubted that she had heard the Don leaving her room the morning after he had carried her up there, unconscious from the blow meant for his brother but which had struck her. He had attended to her with ice-water and a few of his trenchant remarks, then she had fallen asleep and had thought she must be dreaming when a movement distrubed her and what had sounded like the opening and closing of her bedroom door.

There had been no indication from the Don that he spent the night in her room; that was why she had been able to dismiss her suspicion as part of a dream. Why should he stay? She couldn't believe that he felt that concerned about her, so why risk gossip about himself and the resident nurse?

It deeply dismayed her that he had risked such gossip, and the letter from England confirmed that someone had seen him leaving her room and had sent that information to the Sisters of St Anselma. Dominique didn't doubt the poisonous tone of the letter, so she didn't blame the Sisters for doubting her.

It wasn't the first time that someone at the Villa Dolorita had dipped a pen into a venomous pack of lies, and she understood how stricken Candice must have felt when she had been victimised by this malign creature who fed on other people's fears and secrets, distorting the truth into a vicious sort of fantasy.

Dominique could think of only one person who would do such a thing and she knew she was going to have to tackle the Don about it ... and about the way that must be found to clear her name. She sat there watching the sea, alone on the beach but for a few seabirds perched on a rock. Tony had taken Candice for a drive and Dominique had been glad of the opportunity to be by herself.

Her sister had made very good progress in the past couple of weeks, but Dominique hadn't dared as yet to mention Tony's young daughter to her. It was a delicate subject and she wanted Candice in really good shape before she told her about Rosalia.

It was to be hoped that Candice would accept the situation and make a home for the child, but now she was starting to get about again she was talking seriously about opening a dancing school, and Dominique didn't see how a handicapped child could fit into that way of life.

Rosalia was the kind of child who needed a lot of attention, as well as a lot of love, and Dominique didn't think that Candice was cut out to be a surrogate mother. Even if she had children of her own she would no doubt hand them over to a nanny and enjoy their company when she felt in the mood.

A child with special needs like Rosalia would make demands upon a woman's heart as well as her time, and Dominique couldn't see how Tony's problem was going to be easily solved. Her sister's breakdown had proved beyond doubt that her nerves were unreliable, and she didn't really think it would work out even if Candy agreed to the child living with her and Tony.

Dominique sighed and suddenly she wanted to get away from her troubled thoughts, and to forget for a while the disturbing letter from England. She rose to her feet and discarded the robe that covered her bathing suit. She walked barefoot into the sea and welcomed the cool feel of it as she waded out until it reached her shoulders. Quite soon her firm strokes had carried her some distance from the beach, but even though she had left the letter lying there still the words kept beating in her mind and she couldn't seem to escape them.

Oh, why had the Don stayed in her room that night? Whatever had been his motive when he knew what the consequences might be for her if someone saw him leaving and assumed the obvious?

Did she assume that he had felt some concern for her and in watching over her had fallen asleep himself? It had to be that way, and yet she couldn't associate him with any kind of softness where she was concerned. He always dealt with her in such a tough, arrogant way, so it made no sense to her that he should sit at her bedside through the silent watches of the night, being vigilant of Candy's spinster sister.

The outcome was that he had been seen by the pernicious person who knew how to make mischief in a very destructive way. With ice-cold, venomous intention that person had informed the Sisters of St Anselma that Dominique had been visited in the night by her employer . . . it not only sounded tawdry but it contained just enough of a grain of truth to make it digestible.

Dominique had tired herself out with a long swim and now she turned and headed back for the beach, too shortsighed to see that someone was waiting on the sands, a cigar between his teeth. As she started to tread water she noticed him; her immediate instinct was to dive back into the sea, and as if sensing this he took a step forward and had hold of her by the wrist before she could swim away from him.

And then, because the question was so much on her mind, she burst out with it. 'Why did you stay in my room that night? Why did you do such a mad thing?'

For several moments he just looked at her, his grip firm and unbreakable about her wrist, the cigar aggressively held by his teeth. Then he lifted his free hand and removed the cigar, its smoke wafting to her.

'I didn't think you realised that I did stay. You went into a deep sleep, child, and you barely moved all night.'

'All night?' she echoed. 'What were you thinking of—don't you realise that you were seen?'

'Ah, so that's it? Someone has said something?'

'Someone has written to the House of St Anselma and accused me of being your——' She bit her lip. 'You know what I mean.'

'The word is paramour,' he said almost curtly. 'And who is this someone, and how do you know——?'

'How do I know?' She tried to wrest out of his grip, then with a pained look she pointed up the beach to where her robe lay on the sands. 'I've had a letter dictated by the Mother Superior to the Sister who acts as her secretary. It's there in the pocket of my robe—you'd better read it, as you're the cause of it.'

'Come along, then.' He made her go with him, then in frowning silence he digested the contents of the letter, finally refolding it and handing it back to her.

'Well,' he said, almost casually, 'there's a very simple answer to all that, if it so upsets you to have been discovered with a man in your bedroom. You had better allow me to make an honest woman of you.'

Having said this he reclamped the cigar between his teeth and calmly awaited her answer.

'I—I do believe you're mad!' she exclaimed.

'I believe you might be right,' he agreed, his eyes travelling over her as she stood there in the wet and clinging bathing suit, which outlined slender lines and curves usually sedately covered by her navy-blue dress. Her wet hair clung to her neck and her eyes seemed almost silvery in her slim face with the hungry cheekbones. 'But think about it before flying off the handle, you have this urge to sacrifice yourself and I am a man you profess to hate, so we should make a very compatible couple. Think what your life will be with me, all the perks of the *feu sacré* and none of the frustrations of the hair shirt. I shouldn't want you in anything other than a silk shift and the occasional fur right up to those eyes of yours. I have a vivid image of you in both, my dear, but not at same time, of course.'

'Don't!' She backed away from him, from the things he said and the way he looked, his shirt silky black against his dark skin. 'Y-you think it's some kind of joke, don't you, that a poisonous letter has been sent to the Order about me, making me out to be what I'm not.'

'What upsets you the most?' he asked, his eyes narrowed against the smoke of his cigar. 'The fact that people might take you for a young woman with the normal urge to be with a man, or the implication in that letter that you have tarnished your halo?'

'You're being thoroughly beastly,' Dominique flung at him. 'You ought to be as wild as I am that a nasty, insinuating letter has been written about the two of us.

You're a respected man in San Sabina, so what if it gets about that you were seen leaving my room—people always think the worst, don't they? It's human nature.'

'Yes, Dominique. It's human and natural for people to assume that a man and a woman make love when they're alone together, especially in a room with a bed in it. Tell me, would you feel better about all this had I made love to you?'

'*Signore!*'

'You know,' he said thoughtfully, 'I have never seen eyes quite so large as yours, not even here in Italy where the women so often have beautiful eyes. I think if I came a step nearer to you I might fall into those grey eyes, all the way down into the strange, uncertain recesses of what you are.'

'Oh, please——' there was a breathless catch in her voice, 'don't talk in this—this strange way. We have to be practical—I have to ask you to write personally to Mother Superior, assuring her that you only stayed in my room because I—I'd had a bit of an accident and you were a little worried about me. She has to believe you——'

'Has she, Dominique?'

'Well, that was why you stayed—wasn't it?'

'Was it?'

'Of course. Why else would you bother?'

'Why, indeed?' he drawled.

'So—you will write that letter?'

'You really want me to write it?'

'You know I do.'

'In preference to my proposal?'

'Your proposal?' she queried.

'You heard me make it.'

'Oh, but you were making fun of me——'

'The hell I was!'

Dominique gazed at him, seeing him as a whole but not quite seeing the flicker of danger in his eyes. 'Don't be silly,' she said, 'I wouldn't want you to—to propose to me. To go that far. We don't live in Victorian times a-and we both know that nothing happened between us.'

'Not that night,' abruptly he tossed his cigar into a rock pool, 'but it's about to happen now, you damned little English prig! I don't intend to spare your foolish, locked-up virginity a moment longer!'

Swift and tiger-like he had hold of her and the next moment he had flung his arms around her and pulled her to him with ferocious intent, his face devil dark above hers.

'W-what are you doing?' she gasped.

'If you don't know, Dominique, then a large slice of your education needs adjusting. What do you think I'm doing?'

'Behaving very badly—and don't do that!' He was using his mouth to push aside her bathing suit and expose her shoulder.

'Don't you like what I'm doing?' he murmured. 'What soft skin you have—it's about time a man enjoyed touching it, like this.'

As she felt his lips moving over her skin, and felt his hands holding her almost unclad body to his vibrant flesh and bone, she came so painfully awake in those locked-up regions of herself that she could have cried out . . . oh yes, Presidio, kiss me and never stop. Touch me and don't leave a part of me not touched. Love me—*love me*!

The words didn't get said, but that didn't stop her from feeling their stunning impact in her mind, her bones, and the nerve ends which his lips were setting aflame.

'Don't—please,' she begged. He was doing all this to bait her; he had no genuine desire for her but only wished to uncover the yearnings she had bravely concealed. She had come to terms with her undesirability and it was horribly cruel of him to do this to her. She wanted to hate and despise him for it, but her body rebelled against the sensible dictates of her mind and she felt the sensual quiver inside her at the press of his powerful frame and its dominance over her.

'It's cruel of you to do this,' she protested. 'Please stop——'

'With your lips you beg me to stop,' he mocked, 'but your eyes tell a different story. Your eyes lead me on, my strange one, and I want to go where they beckon, into the labyrinth where no other man has been. I believe I might find there a region of flame and drama and melting hot love——'

'Don't—don't say such things!' She struggled to get away from him, but was hopelessly in his power.

'Don't you like to hear them?' he whispered in her ear, his teeth nipping her lobe with little bites.

'I can't bear them.' She quickly turned her head and his mouth became buried in her neck—oh, she had to find a way to make him stop what he was doing. She squeezed her eyes shut, as if not seeing him would stop her from feeling his touch and the deep thud of his heart close to her under the black silk of his shirt, but darkness only intensified sensation and it was as if his kisses were melting through her flesh to her bones where tiny tongues of flame darted back and forth.

'Do you call yourself a gentleman?' It came out as a breathless whisper when she had meant to scornfully shout it.

'Not right now,' he rejoined, his lips tracing her

collarbone, 'if you were hoping to be treated like a lady. Now don't turn your face away, kiss me!'

'I—I'll do no such thing——'

'You will kiss me and like it.' His eyes dominated her and his strong arms held her captive; he quirked an eyebrow as if enjoying her helpless inability to break his hold on her. 'If they won't let you into that nunnery, my dear, then you are going to have to learn to live in the real world. You're going to have to stop being so repressed.'

'I'm nothing of the sort,' she protested.

'Young woman, you are repressed from your ears to your ankles.' He ran his gaze all over her and it was as if his eyes zipped open her swimsuit and exposed her bare white shape to him. 'Don't you think I can tell?'

'Oh, I'm sure you know all there is to know about women,' she said hotly. 'But it's a pity you didn't apply that knowledge to your own fiancée, then perhaps she wouldn't have turned to your brother——' The ghastly words were out and couldn't be unsaid and there washed over Dominique a tide of burning shame at having thrown them in his face. She didn't know what to expect in retaliation and she flinched away from his stillness as if at any second he would become active with a deadly anger.

'That was a nice thing to say, wasn't it?' he said at last. 'I thought you had an angelic nature, but you're as capable of drawing blood as any other woman, aren't you?'

'I'm sorry,' she said huskily.

'Sorry for what you said, or sorry that you've some gall and ginger in you instead of being a plaster saint?'

'I—I've never pretended to be a saint——'

'You could have fooled me, little one.'

'You mean I seem priggish?'

'Very often.'

'I suppose it's a kind of defence.' She swallowed as if to clear the huskiness from her voice, that hint of tears. What a fool she was being, but he had upset the even keel of her emotions and it wasn't fair of him. 'It wouldn't do for someone like me to go around acting like my sister Candy, would it? Anyway, this plain prig of a nurse would appreciate it, *signore*, if you would let go of her.'

'*Santo Dio*, there you go again!' This time he was angry, a flash of ferocity in his eyes as he brought his mouth down on hers and crushed her painfully against him, welding her into him until she was aware of nothing but hot little flames licking through her body and finding their centre where she was a woman and Presidio a man.

How she and he came to be on the sands she didn't know, but suddenly they were there and he was touching her all over and she wanted him never to stop. Her mouth was buried hotly in his shoulder and she could hear him saying things in Italian, and she wanted him saying such secret things almost as much as she wanted him where he was going to be at any moment.

Came a thundering sound . . . it had to be the blood pulsing in her veins, she drowsily told herself.

'*Demonio!*'

The pair of them were soundly drenched as a wave curled over them, quenching their ardent intention and leaving them lying there soaked to the skin.

Suddenly Presidio started to laugh, rising up on his elbow to look down upon Dominique. His eyes were wickedly amused. 'The angels thought fit to put out the fire, *mio amore*, probably just in time!'

It was the tide, and it was coming in high and fast. He leapt to his feet and pulled her up against him. But

suddenly she was struggling to be out of his arms . . .
the cool sobering tide had washed out of her the abandoned longings.

'I—I'll never forgive you!' She tried her utmost to
wrench herself free of the lean hands which now had
steel in them as they held her. 'You had no right to
make me behave in that—way.'

'I made you kiss me, Dominique? I forced you to
put your arms around me, to push your fingers through
my hair and stroke my skin?'

'Damn you!' Tears glittered in her eyes and she
could feel the sea making its way up her legs. 'I didn't
want to have those sort of feelings—what good are they
to someone like me?'

'How angry you make me, child, when you refer to
yourself in that way! By hell, are you obsessed with
being like that sister of yours? What is she supposed to
have that is so precious?'

'She——' tears spilled down Dominique's cheeks,
'she's pretty and lovable a-and I'm not—oh, please
stop what you're doing to me, *signore*. It hurts—it
hurts, you know, to be ridiculed.'

'You believe that's what I'm doing?' He almost spat
the words and his face had never looked so dark. 'I
should break your silly neck for saying such a thing to
me!'

'Go ahead and do it!' She flung back her head to
look right at him, her lashes wet and spiked about the
stormy grey of her eyes. 'Finish off what you've
started—I wouldn't put it past you to have planned
being seen that morning you left my room just so
Mother Superior could be informed that I'm not
suitably moral. Perhaps you thought I could be turned
into the general dogsbody around the place—perhaps
you got together with your brother in the hope that

the old maid would be nanny to his child? After all, Amatrice had her and you were engaged to marry— *oh*!'

Dominique broke off with a cry . . . his fingers were grinding into her shoulder bones as if he meant to crush them.

'How dare you say such things!' His eyes blazed and his black hair was plastered wetly to his forehead. The pair of them were standing knee-high in the rising tide, but nothing seemed to matter except that they throw insults at each other. 'I wouldn't want a bitter old maid like you around my house, least of all in charge of a child! It seems to me that you are riddled with envy of your sister—I wonder why that is? Perhaps Tony's good looks and charm have gone to your head, eh?'

'Perhaps they have,' she flung back. 'He isn't arrogant like you, so it's no wonder your fiancée preferred him! I can quite understand why she used to creep away to be with him—he gave her some tender affection, which is something most women like to be given.'

'You are talking like a chapter out of a magazine,' he said cuttingly. 'It's passion and possession that women want, if they're honest about it. They can get affection from a puppy dog and tender warmth from a woolly vest. Be honest with yourself, Dominique Davis, admit that being down on those sands with me was the most exciting thing that ever happened to you in your life. Admit that you didn't give a single thought to the nunnery while you were murmuring a different sort of incantation in my ears.

'Come on.' He shook her and wasn't gentle about it. 'Confess to the sin of being a normal young woman with the desire to give yourself to a man. You wanted to give yourself to me——'

'No!' she denied, and felt as if something twisted inside her. 'You took unfair advantage of me—you're stronger than I am a-and I couldn't get away from you.'

'That, my dear, is only partly true.' A blatant mockery came into his eyes. 'I'm not a monk, and I know when a woman is on the verge of throwing caution to the wind. Come, you weren't so coy while we lay on the sands and I had my hands all over that soft English skin of yours.'

'Please——' Her lips quivered painfully. 'Don't throw that in my face—you set out to prove that I can be cheap, so just be satisfied that you did it. Now, for what it's worth, you've proved that all women are fundamentally like Amatrice. None of us are angels. I'm sure I've never pretended to be one, it's just that I learned that I wasn't particularly interesting to men and I've come to terms with it. Now, before we both drown, shall we go home?'

'Dominique——' The mockery had gone from his eyes and he had a strange, almost lost look. 'What do I say——?'

'I think, *signore*, that both of us have said enough to last us until I pack my bag and leave the villa. My sister is on the mend. I can't imagine what she'll do about Tony's child, but they'll have to work it out between them. I have my work to go back to. I have that, at least.'

His hands were now weightless on her shoulders and she pulled free of him without much effort . . . what she was feeling inwardly was a conflict of emotion such as she had never felt in her life before. Snatching up her robe, sandals and beach-bag, she paddled through the rising water to the cliffside steps.

Each step as she mounted it was like a bead on a

rosary and each one spelled out a word until she
reached the summit and could string all the words
together into one shattering statement.

It was that she didn't want to love . . . love hurt so
much unless you were accepted just as you were into
the heart of the person you loved. Being left outside
was too cold and lonely . . . it was unbearable, and she
fled along the path through the garden towards the
house. Such a house as she would never see again when
she left it, set within this province of San Sabina where
the air seemed always hung with the scent of citrus
and camphor and dusky cypress.

Dominique knew that impressions of the place
would haunt her, with its village people who only wore
shoes when they went to church. Where the night fish-
ing boats could be seen far down from the villa, their
lanterns flickering on the sea. Here and there among
the rocky outcrops of the hills were little shrines to the
Madonna and Child carved into the rock itself, and
through the warm sunlight came often the sound of
someone singing as he tended the grapevines and the
olive trees. The local wine was still crushed in the stone
troughs by the hardy feet of the workers, the weather-
beaten faces marvellous under tightly bound scarves,
the laughter of the men rich and full.

Rich and full like the grapes, like the sun, like the
music.

Dominique had known nothing of this until she
came to Italy. She had listened to the lessons taught at
the convent while Candice had turned a deaf ear.
Lessons that said hell was eternal if you transgressed
and sinned, that heaven was for those who like the
nuns were chaste and devout and devoted to their
duties.

It wasn't altogether true about heaven . . . she had

learned a different lesson down on the beach in the
arms of Presidio Romanos. They'd have sinned had
the tide not turned, and upon entering her bedroom
Dominique took a long look at herself in the cheval-
glass that reflected her from her bare feet up to her
tangled hair. With shaky hands she found her
spectacles in her beach-bag and put them on.

'Learn another lesson,' she told herself, 'nobody
loves you, so stop thinking about Signor Romanos.
You know what happened meant nothing to him—he
still carries a grudge because of Amatrice and when
he's with a woman, any woman, he gets even with her.
Live with it, accept it, and go home to England where
you belong, Dominique Davis. Go home!'

With resolution she dressed and felt more like herself
once she had on her navy-blue dress and her hair was
combed and sedately knotted. Candice and Tony
would be back from their drive by now and she'd tell
them that she felt her job was finished here and it was
time for her to leave.

With this in mind she sought them out and found
them having tea in the *salone*.

They were having it with a fair-haired little girl in a
white dress with a red ribbon around the waist.
Dominique stood in the doorway of the *salone* and
gazed at her sister, seated there on the big couch
beside the child. She couldn't believe her eyes.

'Nicky, do come in and join us.' Tony rose from an
armchair and came across the room to her; he smiled
at her astonishment. 'We took Presidio's advice and
went to collect Rosalia this afternoon. My brother said
I owed it to Candy to tell her everything myself and
not to put the responsibility on you. He turned out to
be right. Candy agreed that Rosalia should live with
us. Isn't it wonderful?'

'Yes.' Dominique hoped in her heart that her sister would make a success of caring for his daughter. How very pretty she was, with huge dark eyes in contrast to her hair. No wonder Tony loved her and wanted to have her with him.

'Oh, I am pleased!' Dominique went eagerly across to Candice and bent down to kiss her cheek. 'Brave girl, Candy! And may I give Rosalia a kiss?'

The big dark eyes studied her, and then the thin young arms reached up and wrapped Dominique around the waist. For just a second a small flicker of jealousy came into Candy's eyes . . . Dominique saw it and it pleased her. It meant that already Candy felt possessive of Tony's daughter, and it was a promising sign. It told Dominique that she could return to England, safe in the assumption that her sister would try to be a good mother to the little girl who needed all the love she could get.

When Dominique had worked among such children she had learned that love was the best medicine in the world for them . . . for everyone, perhaps.

She had a cup of tea and a cake and casually dropped into the conversation the fact that she was leaving the villa and had decided to go the following day.

'Nicky, you can't go,' Candice protested. 'We want you to stay, Tony and I——'

'My job is over,' Dominique said simply. 'I came here to be your nurse, and now you're better I have to go and get on with my own life.'

'Tony,' Candice appealed to her husband, who was romping on the carpet with Rosalia, 'do tell Nicky that she has no need to go away, especially to put on those drab clothes and become one of those women who never have a home of their own and spend all their days doing good and being holy.'

'If it's what Nicky wants,' Tony said reasonably. 'We can't run her life for her, *carina*.'

'As it happens,' Dominique said quietly, 'I shan't be entering the Order.'

She hadn't known until she said the words that she had decided not to plead her innocence to the Mother Superior. She rather thought that her decision had been made down on the beach where she had learned something about herself which she had refused to face up to. She hadn't the strong, almost martyr-like temperament of the nuns who had been her teachers. She had repressed her natural longings because no one had invited her to share them. And today, with every fibre in her person, she had yearned to share herself with Presidio Romanos.

He didn't want her, but he had shown her that she couldn't take the vows of a nun. She loved a living creature . . . a tall, dark, bittersweet Italian, and she couldn't renounce that love at the altar of the convent. She would guard it like a flame in her heart, but she couldn't quench it, and a nun was required to forsake all earthly joys for those she would eventually find in heaven.

'Well, that's good news,' Tony exclaimed, 'if you don't mind me saying so, Nicky. You aren't cut out for that life—you're far too sweet. You must find a man and marry him. I recommend marriage.'

'Who would have me?' With a smile she rose to her feet, unaware that the westering sun through the long windows lit her hair and played over the delicate shape of her. 'I'm going upstairs now to start packing my bag. And I'm so pleased at the way things have turned out for you both; you will find Rosalia a blessing, I know you will.'

She walked from the *salone* and closed the door on

three people who had found each other and would, with tolerance and love, make a good thing of their lives.

Suddenly tears welled into her eyes and blurred the lenses of her spectacles. She took them off and pressed a Kleenex to the smarting tears; let tomorrow come quickly, for the sooner she faced her departure from the house of Presidio Romanos, the quicker she would get back to work. She would apply for a post in a hospital and work all hours until the man was out of her system; until she had forgotten what his touch felt like on her skin.

She had to forget him physically, but deep in her heart she would lock away his image and wear him there as spinsters often did, having loved and lost the one man they could care for. She belonged in that category of women, she told herself ... the daisies at the wayside that only children sometimes picked and made into a daisy chain.

Dominique smiled a little wistfully as she made her way upstairs ... it was as she reached the landing where her room was situated that a dark shape emerged from the gathering shadows. The shape came swiftly out of the dusk and a blow caught Dominique on the chest, sending her reeling back against the banister rail.

'English trollop!' a voice hissed. 'I will break your neck for you!'

Dominique was struck again, this time in the face so that her spectacles were sent flying. Fingers caught her by the hair and the toe of a shoe struck her painfully in the shin. She found herself grappling with a woman and knew it was Malina. Her heart came into her throat and she couldn't scream though she desperately wanted to ... the woman was mad, it was in her glittering eyes, in her voice and in the ferocious way she was trying to push Dominique down the steep flight of stairs.

A vicious flood of hate poured from the woman's mouth and her fingernails clawed at Dominique's skin, adding pain to the terror. Her mad strength was forcing Dominique to back away, until she was right on the edge of the staircase with its well of hard polished treads behind her, all the way down to the hall.

Dominique tried clinging to the rail and she made a desperate effort to evade the blows that were knocking the breath out of her. 'Mother of Jesus,' she prayed, 'help me! Presidio . . . Presidio, come and save me!'

'Bitch nurse!' Malina swung her arm and had the blow connected with Dominique its hateful force would have sent her toppling backwards, but she lunged to one side just in time and the momentum of the blow unbalanced Malina and with a startled cry she fell head-first down the stairs, where at the bottom she slumped into an abruptly silenced heap, her neck twisted to one side.

Dominique couldn't see this, for her spectacles were somewhere on the floor. All she could do was cling to the stair-rail, breathless and battered and shaking with nerves.

Down in the hall there were voices and lights going on, then all at once someone was leaping the stairs two at a time and the next moment Dominique was dragged into a pair of arms . . . arms that closed so tightly around her that her regained breath was knocked out of her again.

'*Mia cara, mia carissima*, you will tell me that you are all right!' The arms rocked her and lips were all over her face, murmuring and kissing and uttering oaths as the dark eyes took in the scratch marks, a couple of them raking all the way down to Dominique's neck. 'My poor girl, just look at you!'

She was looking at him, at the burning concern in his eyes. *Mia cara*, he called her. *Mia carissima!*

'What happened up here?' he demanded, his lips pressed against her temple, her body pressed hard and safe against his.

'Malina—she tried to—to kill me.'

'Ah, I should have seen it! I should have guessed! It was she who wrote the letters, eh? I thought the woman was showing signs of strangeness, but I told myself it was her time of life and perhaps lack of an occupation. She saved Tony's life, now in a way she has released him from the obligation. It is better so.'

Dominique guessed what he meant and a shudder ran through her. It could so easily have been herself down there on marble floor of the hall, and Presidio must have shared her thought, for his arms convulsively enclosed her.

'The police will come and there will be questions. You are up to facing it, child?'

'I—I think so.'

'A large drink of cognac will steady you.' He swept her up in his arms and as he strode along the gallery he shouted down to those in the hall to cover the wretched woman and phone for the police. He then carried Dominique into the sitting-room of his suite and with a gentleness that shook her heart he lowered her to the big leather couch and placed a cushion behind her head.

For several long moments he just looked at her, then he stroked the hair back from her brow.

'Your poor face,' he murmured. 'First it suffers a punch from me, and now this!'

'Oh well,' she managed a smile, 'it isn't as if I've any beauty to spoil.'

'Who wants to look at a candy-box face all the time?' He cupped her face in his hands and gave her his most dominating look. 'Down on the beach you thought I was playing a game with you, but it was no game, my Dominique. I want you and you have to believe me. I need you quite desperately—and I have never said that to any woman in my life before.'

'There was Amatrice,' she said painfully. 'You think you want me because I'll never behave the way she did—isn't that it, *signore?*'

'By hell no!' He bent his tall head and with a slow deliberation he kissed Dominique's mouth. 'If I have some guilt about her, it's because I should never have agreed to the fool marriage. I agreed because my poor dead parents had arranged it, and I think the girl knew that I found her young and tiresome. I don't happen to find you tiresome, except your talk of being a nun.'

His laughter when he paused held a dark softness. 'You were not meant for that, otherwise fate would not have brought you to my house. Let me quote you some words from Isaiah. *"And I will give thee the treasures of darkness, and hidden riches of secret places."* Let me share those words with you, Dominique. Let them be your vow, *mi amore.* Don't choose the cool cloisters when I invite you to share my warm arms—my love—my life.'

'You mean it?' she whispered. 'Really and truly?'

'I only ever say what I mean, child.'

'Presidio,' she spoke his name huskily, 'I never ever thought anyone would love me.'

'Not boys and blind dolts! Didn't I tell you, they see only the top layer with the pink icing on it, but I see the richness of secret places in you, Dominique. I mean to have you, so you might as well give in to me.'

She smiled, for this was the arrogant Presidio Romanos she knew . . . knew and loved.

'I was going to pack my things and leave in the morning,' she said, daring to tease him.

'I shall lock you in your room—no, correction, I shall lock you in mine.' Holding her gaze with his, he sat down beside her on the couch and with a slow luxuriousness he gathered her into his arms. 'Let us kiss, let us kiss before we have to face the world, *amorevolezza*. Let me tell you that I love your eyes, your sweet kind heart and the whole of you. Let me hear you say that you believe me.'

'I want to believe you, *signore*.'

'Perhaps you need a little persuasion, eh?'

'Try persuading me *a lot*, Presidio.'

'Like this?' He kissed her eyes until they closed drowsily. 'And like this?'

'Mmmmm!' Her arms crept close and loving about his neck. Her heart would not be hung with his image after all, it would be filled with the living, loving, breathing man.

Harlequin Plus
A WORD ABOUT THE AUTHOR

Violet Winspear, who says she began "scribbling' at the age of three, is one of Harlequin's busiest authors. Her first Romance, *Lucifer's Angel* (#593), was published in 1961. Her first presents, *Devil in a Silver Room* (#5), appeared in 1973. She is a member of the select group of authors who have produced more than fifty Harlequins.

Violet's father, who died when she was very young, left her a love of books as a legacy. While still a schoolgirl, she adored inventing stories, and at the age of fourteen she began work at a book bindery. When she turned to writing romances, the author spent more than a year on her first manuscript, working at it in her spare time and sharing her secret with only her mother.

With pride this Harlequin author will tell you that she is a true Cockney, born within the sound of London's Bow Bells. And although she now makes her home at a seaside bungalow, she likes to return to her old haunts in the city's East End and remember the people she knew.

These old friends have walked through the pages of her books in many guises. "And," Violet Winspear confides, "they would have laughed and been slightly embarrassed had I told them they would inhabit Spanish capitals and tropical islands, and marry into the aristocracy!"

FREE!

A hardcover Romance Treasury volume containing 3 treasured works of romance by 3 outstanding Harlequin authors...

...as your introduction to Harlequin's Romance Treasury subscription plan!

Romance Treasury

...almost 600 pages of exciting romance reading every month at the low cost of $6.97 a volume!

A wonderful way to collect many of Harlequin's most beautiful love stories, all originally published in the late '60s and early '70s. Each value-packed volume, bound in a distinctive gold-embossed leatherette case and wrapped in a colorfully illustrated dust jacket, contains...

- 3 full-length novels by 3 world-famous authors of romance fiction
- a unique illustration for every novel
- the elegant touch of a delicate bound-in ribbon bookmark... and much, much more!

Romance Treasury

...for a library of romance you'll treasure forever!

Complete and mail today the FREE gift certificate and subscription reservation on the following page.